CW01457226

Romance Dancer

De-ann Black

Text copyright © 2025 by De-ann Black
Cover Design & Illustration © 2025 by De-ann Black

All rights reserved.
No part of this book may be used or reproduced in any
manner whatsoever without the written consent of the
author.

This is a work of fiction. Names, characters, places,
and incidents are either products of the author's
imagination or are used fictitiously. Any resemblance
to actual persons, living or dead, businesses,
companies, events, or locales is entirely coincidental.

Paperback edition published 2025

Romance Dancer

ISBN: 9798287806774

Romance Dancer is the first book in the Dance, Music & Scottish Romance series set in Scotland.

Dance, Music & Scottish Romance series:
1. Romance Dancer

Also by De-ann Black (Romance, Action/Thrillers & Children's books). See her Amazon Author page or website for further details about her books, screenplays, illustrations and artwork. www.De-annBlack.com

Romance:
Romance Dancer
Summer Ball Weddings & Waltzing
Quilt Shop by the Seaside
Embroidery Bee
Crafting Bee
Scottish Highlands New Year Ball
Ballroom Dancing Christmas Romance
Christmas Ballroom Dancing
Autumn Romance
Knitting & Starlight
Knitting Bee
The Sweetest Waltz
Sweet Music
Love & Lyrics
Christmas Weddings
Fairytale Christmas on the Island
The Cure for Love at Christmas
Vintage Dress Shop on the Island
Scottish Island Fairytale Castle
Scottish Loch Summer Romance
Scottish Island Knitting Bee
Sewing & Mending Cottage
Knitting Shop by the Sea
Colouring Book Cottage
Knitting Cottage
Oops! I'm the Paparazzi, Again
The Bitch-Proof Wedding
Embroidery Cottage
The Dressmaker's Cottage
The Sewing Shop

Heather Park
The Tea Shop by the Sea
The Bookshop by the Seaside
The Sewing Bee
The Quilting Bee
Snow Bells Wedding
Snow Bells Christmas
The Chocolatier's Cottage
Christmas Cake Chateau
The Beemaster's Cottage
The Sewing Bee By The Sea
The Flower Hunter's Cottage
Shed In The City
The Bakery By The Seaside
The Christmas Chocolatier
The Bitch-Proof Suit

Action/Thrillers:

Knight in Miami.   Someone Worse.
Agency Agenda.   Electric Shadows.
Love Him Forever.   The Strife of Riley.

Colouring books:

Summer Nature. Flower Nature. Summer Garden. Spring
Garden. Autumn Garden. Sea Dream. Festive Christmas.
Christmas Garden. Flower Bee. Wild Garden. Flower Hunter.
Stargazer Space. Christmas Theme. Faerie Garden Spring.
Scottish Garden Seasons. Bee Garden.

Embroidery books:

Floral Garden Embroidery Patterns
Floral Spring Embroidery Patterns
Christmas & Winter Embroidery Patterns
Sea Theme Embroidery Patterns
Floral Nature Embroidery Designs
Scottish Garden Embroidery Designs

Contents

CHAPTER ONE

Waltz with me
Sense the rhythm of the dance
When we sweep across the ballroom
It feels like true romance...

Song lyrics played through Dair's mind as he tried to find the right words for the new songs he'd written. Songs he planned to sing and play during his dance tour.

Dair walked through the heart of Edinburgh, highlighted by the glow of the late afternoon sun. Pink and white blossom looked like confetti sprinkled on the trees amid the patches of greenery as he headed towards a niche where the dance studio was situated. The spring flowers and blossom put on a colourful display, creating a sense of romance in the beautiful Scottish city.

His intense turquoise eyes glanced up at the historic structures of the buildings silhouetted against the blue and amber sky, adding a dramatic backdrop to the city.

Classy casual clothes disguised his fit, professional dancer's build, a former ballroom and Latin dance champion. But there was no hiding the way he walked, with long, lithe steps and a rhythmic gait. Not that he was deliberately hiding from anyone. This was his usual attire when heading to the dance studio for rehearsals.

During the depths of the winter he'd been planning his first solo dance tour. He'd performed as part of dance tours in the past, but had never headlined the shows. Now, he'd worked hard to create his own show — the dance choreography, selecting several other dancers to back him and be part of his show. By spring, he'd booked the dance studio for the rehearsals.

Everything was going according to plan, and yet...he knew there were elements missing from the show. It was fine. But fine wasn't great, it wasn't memorable. He wanted to raise the bar, to give audiences throughout Scotland something extra special. Not just dance, but music. He planned to sing and play his own original songs as part of the performances.

The venues, the theatres and halls in Scottish cities and towns were already booked, and tickets were selling well. A company was organising the tour, enabling him to concentrate on the dancing and singing. Romance was at the heart of his show, even though he'd never been lucky in love.

Alisdair, known as Dair, was born and raised in Edinburgh. He was thirty–one, well over six feet, with unruly dark hair that even when cut and styled tended to tumble sexily over his forehead, emphasising his intense blue eyes. A handsome man whose combination of dark brooding looks, sensual smile, and lean, broad–shouldered build, set many women's hearts fluttering. A heartbreaker.

He'd unintentionally broken a few hearts in his time, but he hadn't escaped unscathed. His heart bore the battle scars of romances gone wrong. The most recent, his split with his last girlfriend, and former dance partner, at Christmastime, still cut deep, but their relationship was over, and working on his new dance show had helped him leave that part of his bitter past behind.

But in the quiet of the night, when he was alone in his house situated in the outskirts of Edinburgh, he hoped one day to find the woman for him, to bring real romance into his world.

Blinking against the glare of the afternoon sun, he hoisted his large bag up on his shoulders and walked towards the dance studio that catered for theatre rehearsals as well as dance.

The studio was fairly new, barely a few months old since it's successful opening. It comprised of two main rooms — a spacious dance room with a mirrored wall and barre for stretching, and a second room with adequate floor space for dancing, plus a stage. A few other small rooms in the studio facility were available for hire too. Dair had hired the dance room to rehearse the choreography. His forthcoming show was due to go on tour throughout cities and towns in Scotland.

Dair disappeared inside the studio's small reception, leaving the exciting bustle of Edinburgh behind, and stepped into the world he was familiar with — dancing.

A poster advertising Dair's dance show was pinned to the reception's notice board. He was pictured in one of his stylish poses, wearing dark trousers emphasising his long legs, and a white Scottish ghillie shirt with the neck laces undone, exposing a hint of his strong, lean–muscled chest.

Two people were talking to the receptionist, making a booking to hire a room, and Dair swept by and through to the narrow corridor that separated the dance room from the studio room.

The door to the dance room was closed, but not locked. As he approached it, he noticed that the stage room door opposite was open, and he slowed down to peek in at the stage play rehearsal. A dress rehearsal he assumed, as the actors on stage were in costume. The clothes were from a bygone era.

The stage director held a script and stood down in front of the stage prompting the actors. The man had an authoritative manner and a voice that hinted he was an actor himself, or had been. In his mid–thirties, fairly tall, good–looking, he was well–dressed in muted classics, including a pinstripe shirt, tie, and waistcoat.

Shrugging the bag from his shoulders, feeling the warmth of the premises, Dair took his heavy jacket off, revealing his lean muscles in a white, racer back vest and dark training trousers, while quietly watching the actors perform.

The stage director prompted them several times, and Dair noted the nuances in their dialogue. He thought the dialogue was excellent. He'd seen the play's poster on the notice board in passing a few times, but hadn't taken in the details of the leading actors or the director.

The words sounded poetic, intense, intriguing and romantic. Maybe that's what was missing from his own show — he'd certainly struggled to write the lyrics for his two new songs. He could dance. He could sing and play the piano, keyboards and guitar. But he wasn't a writer.

'Tickets for the play are on sale.' A woman's voice sounded behind him in the quiet corridor.

Dair jolted, and glanced round to find her beautiful pale grey eyes staring at him, accusing him of watching the play's rehearsals when he had no business doing so.

Elegance personified, she wore a silvery grey blouse and charcoal trousers, and even in her heels, she barely came up to his shoulders. Slightly younger than him, her slender figure had poise, and there was a confidence in her manner that made him assume she was one of the actors. A starring role. She had leading lady quality, and a timeless beauty with lovely alabaster skin. Her blonde hair hung in soft waves around her shoulders, and she was holding a cup of tea. Presumably, she'd popped out to get this while the play's rehearsals continued. And caught Dair peering into the stage room on her way back.

'The dates probably clash with my own show.' Dair had seen that the play began in the summer, and so did his tour.

The grey eyes looked at him, unimpressed.

Inwardly, she hid her reaction to seeing the raw masculinity standing in front of her, causing her heart to flutter. Mentally scolding herself, she took a deep breath.

'Excuse me, Dair.' She walked past him into the stage room and closed the door behind her with a curt finality.

Dair stood for a moment, feeling her reproach. He didn't know her name, but his first impression of this young woman made him want to find out. If she was the play's leading lady, or one of the lead actors, she'd be listed on the show's website. Grabbing his bag and jacket, he hurried into the dance room, dumped his things on a chair, dug his phone out and proceeded to check the website. He knew the name of the show from the poster.

Scrolling through the details, he saw a picture of the stage director, Cambeul, and the main actors involved. But no elusive young woman.

The sound of lively voices made him click his phone off and welcome in the dancers arriving for the rehearsal.

'Everything okay, Dair?' one of the men said. 'You look rattled.'

'I'm fine, just thinking about the choreography,' Dair lied.

The cheery chatter continued as the dancers did their warm–up stretches.

And the rehearsals began.

Dair waved them off after two hours of intensive choreography finished on an uplifting note. He was still working on the new choreography, honing it, seeing what worked well, watching their performances in the mirrors.

After they'd gone, Dair rehearsed on his own, and frowned at his mirror image that lacked the drama, the power and the sense of romance he'd envisaged.

He planned to work on the choreography at home where he had a makeshift dance floor in the large living room of his house, a two–storey, traditional mansion, set within gardens and surrounded by trees for privacy. The family home. Dair came from money. And was wealthy in his own right. His parents were off travelling the world, on holiday, on business, as they often did, leaving him free to dance into the late–night hours, practising his skills.

Eventually, Dair picked up his bag and headed out of the dance room, just in time to see Cambeul walk out of the now empty stage room, the last to leave.

Taking the opportunity to talk to the stage director, Dair approached him.

'Excuse me, Cambeul. Can I have a quick word?'

Cambeul was suited, wearing a jacket over his shirt and waistcoat. He tucked a copy of the script in his case. 'Yes, Dair,' he said, acknowledging he knew his name too.

'There was a woman I met earlier,' Dair began. 'She seemed to be part of the play. I checked the show's website, but I didn't see her photograph on the cast list.'

Cambeul frowned. 'All the actors are pictured, along with key members of the play. What did she look like?'

'Beautiful, blonde hair, grey eyes—'

'Ah, that's the playwright, Huntine Grey.'

7

'She wrote the play you're directing?' Dair wanted to clarify.

'Her name is listed, but we haven't put a picture up, not yet,' Cambeul explained. 'Why do you ask?'

Dair summarised what happened earlier.

Cambeul smiled. 'We're not supposed to snoop into each other's rehearsals, but I'm sure you won't tell anyone about our new costumes. We like to release pictures of these ourselves to promote the show. The costumes for this play are rather special. Vintage quality, ideal for the story as it's set in the past.'

'I overheard some of the dialogue. Quite poetic. And you sounded as if you were an actor yourself.'

'I was, still am on occasion. Mainly, I've moved into directing, which suits me. Huntine's script is excellent. This is her third stage play to be performed. Quite a talent.'

Dair heard the admiration in Cambeul's tone that resonated in the quiet corridor.

'Indeed,' Dair agreed.

Cambeul continued to show his admiration. 'Huntine Grey is a playwright, novelist, poet and lyricist.' He smiled. 'I call her a *wordsmith*.'

'Song lyrics?' Dair wanted to clarify.

'Yes, though I've no idea of the details, only that she'd written lyrics for songs in the past when she worked at a music recording studio. But now she concentrates on her plays and romance novels.'

'Is she from Edinburgh?' Dair had heard a hint of the Highlands in her voice.

'No, she's based on the west coast, Glasgow. She's here in Edinburgh for the play's rehearsals. She'll head back to Glasgow once the play begins. But Huntine is originally from the Scottish Highlands. Her parents live up there. They named her after a small niche in the Highlands.'

'You seem to know her quite well,' Dair remarked.

'Someone as special as Huntine is worth knowing.'

Dair picked up on more than mere admiration for her. Were they dating?

'Thank you,' said Dair. 'Perhaps I'll meet her again soon.'

Cambeul smiled tightly, taking in the fit–looking potential rival. 'Good luck with your dance show.'

Dair smiled, and then Cambeul hurried away, leaving Dair pondering whether Huntine Grey had a website. And whether she would be willing to help him with his new song lyrics.

Huntine and Cambeul had dinner in an upmarket restaurant not far from the dance studio. He'd booked a table for two that offered a view of the glittering lights of the city. After discussing the play's rehearsal from earlier that afternoon, he broached on another subject.

'The dancer, Dair, was interested in chatting to me today — *about you*,' he revealed.

Huntine looked across at him. Cambeul's hazel eyes hinted that he had something secretive to tell her.

Cambeul cut into his dinner, leaving his comment dangling in the air.

'What did he want to know?'

'He thought you were one of the actors, but couldn't find you listed and pictured on the show's credits.' Cambeul took a sip of his drink. 'He described you as *beautiful*. I got the distinct impression that your brisk encounter intrigued him. I told him you were the playwright, Huntine Grey.'

'Anything else?' she prompted him, sensing there was more to tell. She'd known Cambeul since he'd directed her first play a few years ago, and had learned that he liked to add drama to his conversations that rarely merited it.

'I described you as a wordsmith. Told him you were a playwright, novelist and poet. But he was particularly interested when I added *lyricist*. I said you'd written song lyrics in the past during your work for a music recording studio.'

'Why would a dancer like him be interested in my song lyrics?'

Cambeul shrugged and swept a hand through his well–cut, light brown hair. 'Perhaps he has aspirations to be a singer or songwriter.'

The conversation ended without resolution regarding Dair's interest in Huntine, and swung back to the topic of the play.

'I thought the costumes were marvellous,' Cambeul enthused.

'They were,' she agreed, while her thoughts still drifted to Dair.

Cambeul glanced over at her, offering a piece of advice. 'Be careful of becoming inveigled in Dair's ambitions.'

'I have no intention of doing so,' she heard herself say, while unable to shake off the effect he'd had on her. Dair was a heartbreaker, and the last thing she needed was another broken heart on top of the one that hadn't yet mended from the break–up with her last boyfriend.

She thought she'd chosen wisely, a man outwith the theatre and entertainment industry. An accountant working in finance in Glasgow. But she hadn't accounted for him cheating on her with his previous girlfriend and getting back together with his ex. Huntine's trust and her heart had been ripped to shreds. She was still mending. She believed she would, but it would take time. Working on her play, and her new romance novel was what she needed. Not indulging in a hot summer fling with the handsome dancer. Flings weren't her style. Romance was.

'...and I thought the stage lighting for the end of Act One was perfect.'

Huntine stirred from her faraway thoughts, and jumped back into the conversation. 'The blue lighting created an atmosphere of a cold, nighttime effect in the city.'

'I could almost feel the chill in the air as the lovers walked off stage,' said Cambeul. 'I adore scenes like that. You've written another great play dripping with drama and romance.'

Dair drove through the city to the outskirts where trees overarched the entrance to the mansion's gardens. He parked outside the front door and carried his training bag inside.

Running upstairs, he put his bag down in his bedroom and hung up his jacket. Then he hurried back down to the living room and turned on the lamps that gave a warm glow to the stylish surroundings.

Ideas for the choreography played in his thoughts and he wanted to try out the new routine.

Flicking on some music, he began to dance, interpreting the song, one of the songs that was part of the dance show. Most of the songs were popular tunes, and the show's tour director had these lined up.

Dair danced until he was happy with the new routine. It felt closer to what had been eluding him. Strong, dramatic, romantic.

It was late at night when he finally took a shower, put on a pair of silky boxers and climbed into bed.

Thoughts of Huntine played in his mind, until he finally gave in, picked up his phone from the bedside table, and in the semi–shadows of the nightglow shining in the window, he checked out her website.

Classy, contemporary, Huntine's website listed her plays and novels, along with brief synopses of the storylines. Romance was at the heart of them.

Several photos of her made him pause and study her face and those eyes that had looked at him with scorn. She wasn't an actress, nor had been. Her world was words. Maybe she'd help him with the lyrics that were proving to be elusive. He'd written the music, and had some lyrics, but perhaps she could add that special touch to the lyrics.

Daring to hope, he sent her a brief message via her website.

Dear Miss Grey,

I'd like to talk to you about helping me write lyrics for my new songs.

Can we chat?

It was nice meeting you today at the studio. I hope we can meet again there soon. My next rehearsal is scheduled for two nights from now.

He listed the times, suggesting they meet before or after the dancing.

Dair.

He added his own website and phone number.

Settling down to sleep, he wondered when she'd read his message and if she'd reply.

Huntine closed her laptop at almost two in the morning, after another late–night writing, working on her new book and making notes for her next play.

Her phone showed she'd received a website message from Dair.

She read it and replied.

I don't write song lyrics these days.

I concentrate on my romance novels and plays.

Then she settled down to get some sleep.

She'd rented a small flat in Edinburgh in a building where the walls were old and solid and cut out the noise of the city, of people. The quietude suited her. She preferred to write without chatter or music, especially any songs with lyrics as the words interfered with the dialogue playing in her thoughts as she wrote about her fictional characters.

Snuggled up in the cosy quiet of her bedroom, her phone lit up with a message. She read the reply from Dair.

I understand.

All the best with your new play.

She clicked her phone off, glad that he'd accepted her reply.

Dair ate breakfast in his kitchen the following morning. He added fresh raspberries to his bowl of porridge and poured milk on top. Earlier, he'd done his usual exercise routine, a warm–up comprising of stretches, followed by free weights and core strength exercises to keep his physique strong.

There were no rehearsals at the dance studio over the next two days, but he planned to work from home, practising new ideas for the choreography, and for his song lyrics.

Finishing breakfast, he went through to the living room and opened one of the patio doors to let the fresh, spring morning air in. Pale sunlight tried to force its way through the trees, and he sat down at his piano in a corner of the room that had a view of the garden through the glass patio doors. The spacious gardens surrounded by trees enabled him to play without disturbing others.

The notes he'd scribbled from his previous session were still propped up on the music stand where he'd left them on the piano. He'd written new lyrics while tinkling out the tune on the classical baby grand piano.

His parents could both play the piano, and he'd learned from them since he was a boy. And he played keyboard. The guitar was something he'd picked up along the way, and now he played both his acoustic and electric guitars proficiently.

The piano, keyboard and guitars played important roles in his songwriting, offering him different musical perspectives.

There was one song he'd finished months ago, and he intended to include it in the dance tour. The two new songs were still missing all the lyrics, though he'd written the music.

The other dancers taking part in his tour knew he could sing and play, though none of them were skilled musicians, only accomplished dancers.

Dair's dance show tour director was keen to showcase the new songs, and promote Dair's singer–songwriter talent as well as his dancing.

The tour director had ascertained that a few of the theatres had pianos available for Dair to play on stage, and those venues that didn't, he could use his keyboard that was handily portable to take to the shows. Dair would also play his guitars at the performances.

Sitting at the piano, he began to play and sing the lyrics he'd written.

Words were not his forte. He wished he was a wordsmith like Huntine Grey. The best he could do was write from the heart, and hope he could express the emotion he felt when he played the music.

CHAPTER TWO

I'm in step with you
You're in step with me
We share the rhythm of the dance
And the romance —
Romantic dancers...

The next dance rehearsal night went well, and after the dancers left, Dair lingered to practise a few moves on his own, viewing himself in the mirror to gauge the choreography.

He'd just finished, and taken his top off to reveal his bare chest when a voice spoke to him from the dance room's doorway.

'What type of songs do you sing?'

Seeing Huntine reflected in the mirror, Dair started to sing before turning around and walking towards her. His long, slow, strides were emphasised by the black training trousers he wore that fitted the contours of his lean–muscled thighs.

She stood in the doorway, standing her ground while her heart reacted to the raw masculinity walking over to her. It was her own fault for interrupting him, uninvited.

The rich tones of his musical voice reverberated through the room, and through her, stirring senses she'd put on ice to concentrate on her career. No man had made her feel like this in a long, long time.

Stay calm, she told herself.

Dair's voice filled the air with a melody she'd never heard before. One of his own songs she assumed. It had a memorable quality to it. The lyrics were fine, and he hummed the lines and phrases that were missing without skipping a beat of the song.

Now standing right in front of her, he finished singing the chorus, or was it the verse? She wasn't sure. But she was certain that her telltale blush showed the feelings his song, his voice, and Dair stirred in her.

The last note lingered for a second and then faded into the silence between them before Huntine spoke up, keeping her voice steady.

'One of your own melodies?'

Dair's turquoise eyes gazed down at her and he nodded. 'I'm still working on the lyrics.'

He didn't repeat his previous request for her help. She'd told him no. Though he was hopeful she'd reconsidered.

She looked even more beautiful than when he'd first met her. Standing there in the doorway, lit by the bright glow of the dance room lights.

He turned around and walked over to his holdall and dug out his notebook containing his lyrics.

The broad muscles of his back tapered down to his fit torso, and his smooth skin added to his handsome appearance. Dair was a looker. No doubt about that.

'These are my scribbles.' He held his notebook out, encouraging her to come in and take it.

Huntine stepped into the room and walked over to him. She wore a silky white shirt, grey jeans and pumps. Her blonde hair fell casually around her shoulders. And her rose pink lipstick emphasised her soft lips, while her makeup was neutral, understated.

Accepting the notebook, she skimmed through it, thinking that his method of writing was nothing like hers. His was jotted in bullet–points. Hers was organised, lines finished.

His heart took a hit when those gorgeous pale grey eyes of hers looked up at him as she handed back the notes.

'How many songs need lyrics?'

'Two.' He flicked to the notes on the first song. 'This one has a couple of verses, but I'm stuck with the chorus lyrics. And the second song has a chorus, but I can't find the right words to express the music.'

'Was that the song you were singing?'

'Yes.' He sighed heavily. 'I can dance what I feel, but I can't find the lyrics to match.'

Huntine took the notebook back off him, and unclipped the pen attached. 'Dance it.'

'I have a recording I made.' He scrolled through his phone to find it. 'It's rough. I made it yesterday at home playing the piano. I've recorded the other song on guitar.'

'You're a musician?' She sounded impressed.

He nodded, and then she heard his exquisite piano playing. The song's introduction was dramatic.

'I'm happy with the musical intro,' he said.

'You should be. It's excellent. What type of piano do you play?' The wonderful tone of the classic piano sounded clear even on the phone recording.

'A baby grand. Do you play?'

18

Huntine shook her head. 'Not at all. I just write lyrics.'

'We're a perfect match.'

His comment jarred her, and she glanced at him.

'I write the music. You write the lyrics,' he clarified. 'Two pieces merging perfectly as one.' His elegant fingers clasped together for emphasis.

There was something in his gesture that messed with her calm emotions, and she pushed the feelings aside to concentrate on his song.

Dair's voice now sang the first verse.

She smiled when he filled in the gaps with la–la–la notes where the lyrics were missing.

This was the first time he'd seen Huntine smile. His heart took another hit, deeper this time, with a warning that she wasn't his type, and yet clearly she affected him in ways he wasn't sure how to handle. He sensed the barriers were up and that she wasn't looking for romance, and wasn't attracted to him. He could tell when a woman was keen on him. And he could tell by the way Huntine wasn't looking at him.

If she was going to help him with his lyrics, it was probably better this way, to keep their relationship on a business level.

Dair rewound the song, turned the volume up, sat the phone down, dimmed the brightness of the lights, creating a more intimate atmosphere, and then walked to the centre of the floor.

He struck a strong, dramatic pose as the intro played — and then he danced.

Huntine watched, feeling the power of his balletic and athletic moves as he spun, jumped and danced around the floor. She'd seen dancers perform live on stage, but never had she experienced anything like this, seeing him up–close, feeling the air whip past her as he swept around the room. The powerful leaps, pirouettes performed with such precision she hardly dared to blink so she wouldn't miss a moment of it.

And then, while caught in Dare's world of dance, she heard ideas for lyrics that expressed what she was watching, what he was expressing.

She quickly wrote down the lyrics, rhymes that sprang to mind.

And by the time the song ended, and Dair finished facing the mirror in a dynamic pose, she'd written the chorus, the four lines he needed for the song.

He saw her in the mirror, writing in the notebook, and then she glanced up and held it out for him to read.

Dair smiled and nodded as he read the lyrics. 'We are the perfect match.' He studied her. 'Why did you change your mind to help me?'

'I kept getting snippets of lyrics filtering through my thoughts. That happens to me sometimes. When I'm writing one thing, words for some other project come to mind. At first, I refused to write them down, knowing that if I started, I'd probably be tempted to become involved in writing your lyrics. Then I thought...maybe it's only a few lines, a verse, a chorus. And I like a challenge.'

The broad shoulders tilted gently in front of her. 'You think I'm a challenge.'

'I do,' she said without any hesitation. 'At least, I believe your song lyrics are. I need to be sure that my words are a suitable fit for your songs. The meanings behind the words have to elevate your music. Enhance the songs.'

They agreed to work together on the songs. 'I'll have an agreement drawn up so that you'll be fairly paid for your lyrics,' he promised.

'I need to continue with my own writing while creating the lyrics,' she emphasised. 'I've started work on my next play, but I want to see the audience reaction to the new play before I write too deep. I'm mainly writing my latest romance novel. I have a deadline for the book. But I write fast. I always have.'

'And work into the wee small hours,' he said.

'I get a lot written in the depths of the night. After dinner, I can finish a chapter if I work until well after midnight.'

'Doesn't that interfere with your romantic life?' He'd noted that Cambeul called her Miss Grey, and there was no diamond sparkling on her ring finger. He was fishing for information that was none of his business, and yet...he dared to mention this.

'No.' Her one–word reply told him nothing, not even in the tone of her voice.

Her guard was obviously up, and he didn't venture to pry.

Instead, he swung the conversation back to the dancing. 'Did you see any of the rehearsal this evening?'

She shook her head. 'I waited until the dancers came out after your rehearsal. Then I heard the music and assumed you were practising on your own for a wee while. When the music finished, I came through to talk to you.' Though she didn't expect to find him shirtless.

'Would it help you to write the lyrics if you saw some of the choreography?'

'It would. When is your next rehearsal slot?'

Dair scrolled through his phone. 'Not for another few days. The studio is heavily booked, but we have our rehearsal schedule worked out well.' He found what he was looking for, and stepped closer. 'I record the choreography so that I can go over it later, hone the steps, the movements.'

Huntine was keen to view the footage.

'This was from tonight's rehearsal.' Dair stood close to her while he held the phone so that they could both view the dancing.

She was aware again that she barely came up to his shoulders, and could feel the masculine energy from him. Some would call it *star quality*, that potent element that added to his talent as a dancer.

'As you can see, there are three couples dancing here, plus my leading lady dancing with me,' he explained. 'Shona and I danced competitively a few times in the past. Then we had a bit of a personal split.'

'You dated?' It was her turn now to fish for information.

'No. The attraction was one–sided. I admire Shona's dancing. She's an excellent dancer and a suitable partner, but I didn't want any romantic entanglement.'

Huntine got the message.

'But we recently put the past behind us to dance together on the tour. When she heard that I was headlining my own dance show, she came back to patch things up,' he added.

Huntine noticed that the choreography was rather like Dair's lyrics, unfinished, though the plans for the tour were well ahead.

'The choreography is often taken right up to the wire in preparation for a dance tour,' he explained. 'It keeps it fresh, and allows for new elements to be added, or taken out. The dancers are all professionals and can pick up the changes to the choreography really well.'

'I noticed that you're touring all eight cities in Scotland,' she said.

'Yes, and Scottish towns, and one of the islands off the west coast. When the tour was announced, tickets started to sell quite well, and dates and venues have been added. But we're only touring Scotland. I hope you'll come and see some of the performances.'

'If our schedules allow,' she said. Then she turned her attention back to the recording on his phone. 'I recognise these songs.' They were popular hits from the past.

'The majority of the songs for the show are well–known,' Dair explained. 'The tour director and I have these organised. But three of my own songs will be added that I'll perform.'

'Ah, there you are, Huntine,' Cambeul called into the room, interrupting them. 'We're about to rehearse the scene for the beginning of Act Three.'

'I'll be right there,' Huntine told him.

Dair and Cambeul gave each other a stilted nod of acknowledgment, and then the director hurried away.

'Send me a copy of your lyrics,' she said to Dair. 'I'll see what I can come up with and get back to you.'

'Thanks again for agreeing to help.'

Huntine nodded and walked through to the stage room, leaving Dair with a feeling that was hard to shake off. He would've liked to have spent more time with her.

Cambeul clasped a copy of the script as the actors took their places on stage to begin Act Three. Huntine sat down and joined him.

The stage lights dimmed and the two lead actors began...

'Has shirtless Dair inveigled you into his business?' Cambeul whispered to Huntine.

'I'm writing his song lyrics. That's all.'

'I thought you were busy with your novel.'

'I am, but it's just a few lyrics. The contrast of writing always sparks new ideas for me. It'll probably help with my book.'

Cambeul pretended he was discussing the script with Huntine. 'You're not dancing with him?'

'No. I haven't mentioned anything about my dancing. And I'd rather you didn't either.'

'My lips are sealed.' Cambeul sat back, without another word, and watched the actors perform on stage.

Dair had put a top on and was packing up his bag when Shona walked in.

'I left my dance shoes.' She went over to where they were tucked under a chair at the side of the room, and put them in her holdall.

Shona was the same age as Huntine, but slightly taller. She had a slender, toned figure. Her shiny, dark auburn hair was swept back in a ponytail, and her blue eyes studied Dair. 'Were you practising new moves?'

'I was. But it's late, so I'm heading home now.'

'Can you drop me off at my flat?'

Dair slung his bag over his shoulder. 'Yes.'

'Great.' Shona led the way out.

The drive was a short one and not on his route home. Shona did most of the talking, trying to encourage him to compete with her again in forthcoming dance contests. One contest in particular, due around the time that the tour began.

'I'm not stepping back into the competitive circuit,' he said. 'You know that.'

'Yes, but, surely you miss the buzz of it. We could win, or place well in this next contest. It would be a great title to have as a credit.'

He pulled up and parked outside her flat. 'You'll need to find someone else to partner with for the competitions. All my energies are on the dance tour.'

She sat back in the seat. 'What will you do when the tour's finished?'

'Plan the next one.'

Sighing heavily, she opened the door, stepped out and then leaned down to issue a parting shot. 'I've received a couple of offers for other dance projects that I'm planning to discuss soon.'

'I hope they work out well for you. But for now, we have to concentrate on the tour. And not squabble.'

'I'm not squabbling,' she snapped at him, and then took a deep breath. 'I'll see you at the next rehearsals.' Her ponytail swished as she walked away.

He waited to see that she got in safely, and then drove off home.

Dair sat at his piano at home the next day working on his songs, playing and singing the lyrics of the chorus Huntine had written for him. The words flowed well, and he liked them.

He was about to stop for lunch when Huntine phoned.

'I've written more lyrics. I watched the choreography video again and hopefully you like what I've come up with.'

Dair checked his messages and skimmed the lyrics she'd sent him. Two new verses, and she'd reworked some of his previous lyrics.

'Late night?' he said.

'Early morning. I'm not just a night owl.'

'Clearly. These are great. I'm at my piano right now. I could try them out or...I was going to make lunch. Want to join me?'

'A working lunch?'

'Is there any other kind in our world?' he joked with her.

'Fairly true,' she agreed. Then she considered his offer. 'Okay, give me your address.'

He told her and then added, 'Do you like pasta?'

'I do. See you soon.'

Huntine drove to Dair's house. It wasn't too far, and she admired his traditional mansion set in the well–kept gardens. Parking outside the front door, she knocked, but getting no reply, she wandered around to the back of the house to the kitchen.

She wore smart casuals, dark trousers, and a cream wool coat over a cream blouse. Her hair and makeup were stylishly understated, and her laptop was in a bag slung over her shoulder.

Dair was busy in the kitchen, singing and gyrating while he prepared the pasta, unaware that she was watching him through the window. He'd rolled up the sleeves of his white shirt, and seemed adept at cooking while performing his own type of kitchen cabaret.

Waving to attract his attention, she smiled to herself as he still didn't notice her. Cooking, singing, dancing, she was entertained by his antics.

He drained the pasta into a large serving dish and mixed in a rich tomato and spicy vegetable sauce.

Waltzing over to where he'd chopped tomatoes and greentails, he then stirred the tomatoes through the pasta and sprinkled the greentails on top.

Huntine tapped on the window, alerting him she was there, and startling him.

He opened the kitchen door and she stepped inside. The large kitchen's colour scheme was white and pale lemon. Gleaming pots and pans hung on the walls.

'I knocked on the front door but—'

'Sorry, I didn't hear you. I was so busy cooking lunch.'

And singing and dancing she thought. 'It smells delicious.'

'Put your coat and bag through in the living room while I serve it up.' He gestured in the general direction.

Huntine wandered through to the living room, draped her coat on the back of a chair and put her bag down. A quick glance around showed a stylish room with musical touches.

'Sit down, tuck in,' he said as she walked back into the kitchen. He'd set two plates of pasta on the table and was making the tea. 'How do you like your tea?'

'Strong, with milk.'

Dair poured two cups of tea and brought them over to the table.

'Thank you for this.' She tried a mouthful of the pasta, and nodded.

'I enjoy cooking, though I don't always have time, especially when I'm busy with the dancing.'

'I've been eating out a lot while I'm here. I cook when I'm at home in Glasgow.'

'How long are you staying in Edinburgh?'

'Until the opening of the play, probably for the first week of the performances. Then I'll head back to the west coast.'

'Cambeul said that you're originally from the Highlands.'

'I am, though I spent a lot of time in Glasgow with my grandparents. School holidays, weekends, whenever my parents were busy with work. My father travelled around a lot on business and my mother usually went with him. I was happy to stay with my grandparents. It was always a wonderful adventure.'

'An adventure?' Dair prompted her.

'My grandfather was a theatre manager. That's where he first met my grandmother. She was a dancer performing on stage at one of the shows. They met, fell in love, and lived theatrically ever after. Or so they like to joke about it. I enjoyed visiting the theatre, watching the shows, seeing everything that went on backstage, the costumes, the scenery.'

'So this was where you got your love of the theatre and plays.'

Huntine nodded. 'I always wanted to be a writer. My short stories were published in school magazines when I was a wee girl. I illustrated the stories too. And wrote poems.'

'Published from an early age,' he summarised. 'That must've been very encouraging.'

'It was.' She smiled and gestured around. 'Now here I am with you, to discuss your lyrics for songs you'll perform on stage.'

'The lyrics you wrote last night work so well with the music.'

'I'm pleased.'

They tucked into their lunch.

'Beautiful piano,' she commented, having seen it in the living room.

'I'll play after lunch, let you hear the lyrics.'

'I'd like that.'

They continued to eat their lunch and chat about their respective businesses. Then Dair cleared the plates away and they went through to the living room to work on the songwriting.

CHAPTER THREE

You make me remember what I could be
With you I recall the past
When I dance with you I feel free
I know our love will last...

One of the patio doors in the living room was open and the scent of the spring flowers in the garden wafted in. A cherry tree covered with pink blossom draped its branches close to the house and some of the petals were sprinkled over the grass like bridal confetti.

Huntine wandered across the polished wooden floor that he used to practise his dancing, and breathed in the fresh air. 'This is such a lovely room to use when you're working on your music and dancing.'

'I'm fortunate.' Dair sounded as if he didn't take it for granted. 'It's an extraordinary balance of extremes. Performing to audiences, working with other dancers, and the whole social life that goes with it, contrasts so starkly with the time I'm here on my own. Playing guitar and piano, and dancing. Though I'm sure a creative person like you would understand.'

Huntine stood gazing out at the daffodils, crocus and primroses. 'I do, though obviously I'm behind the scenes, not centre stage like you.'

'But you're in the buzz of the theatre during the rehearsals, and when your plays fill a theatre with an audience anticipating the drama.'

'That's true.' She walked over to him as he sat down at his piano and let his fingers drift across the keys, warming up, ready to play one of the songs, and sing her lyrics.

The tone of the piano resonated through the room, and her own anticipation rose up as he set the lyrics on the stand in front of him.

She stepped back, walked over to the couch and sat down, ready to take in his performance.

Dair began to play, and then sang the lyrics.

Hearing them for the first time, sung live, played with such feeling, a rush of emotion swept over her.

His fingers brushed over the keys, playing the notes that ended the chorus.

He stopped and looked over at her. 'What do you think?'

Huntine was writing in her notebook, hearing his voice, but giving priority to the new lyrics that had been prompted by his playing.

Dair didn't interrupt, and waited until she'd stopped writing at speed.

She lowered her pen and smiled at him.

'More lyrics?' he surmised.

'Yes. Four lines.' She stood up and took the notebook over to him.

He propped it up on the stand and started playing.

'These are for a verse,' she said. 'I think some of the verses could be interchanged, depending on the story they're telling.'

The notes tinkled from the piano and Dair tried out the lyrics, singing them as he read the words. Then he stopped suddenly.

'Something wrong? I'm happy to rework them,' she offered.

'No, quite the opposite.' Dair stood up. 'This could be the missing verse I've been looking for.' He took a deep breath. 'It was one of those feelings...I didn't know exactly what I wanted, until I heard these words.'

'You want to use this for the song's first verse.'

Dair was now striding over to where his pale blue electric guitar was set up on a stand. He plugged it in, and slung the strap over his shoulders.

'Not for the song I was playing on piano. Another song. The dance show's first number. I play the opening riff on electric guitar.'

Dair warmed up, strumming the strings, adjusting the tone, playing a few chords until he was happy with it.

She had yet to hear this song and sat down while he got ready.

He stilled the strings. Took a moment to breathe. And then he began to play the opening riff, filling the room with the astounding resonance of the electric guitar.

From looking like a classical pianist, with his open–neck shirt and sleeves rolled up, Dair now bore a sensual quality that stirred her to the core.

The electric guitar intro created a frisson of excitement in the air.

And then Dair put the guitar aside, sat down at the piano, and sang the first verse, glancing at the new lyrics, picking up the words she'd written that captured the emotion of the song.

He looked over at Huntine to gauge her reaction, and seeing her smile, he continued to play the piano.

The chorus had words missing, and his la la la, filled the gaps.

The second verse went well with the first verse and the chorus. Huntine now understood why he wanted her lyrics for this song. The theme of romance was strong, dramatic, and suited it.

For a moment, she caught a glimpse of how exciting it would be when he played this song to open his show.

'I play piano for the remainder of the song and the outro. This leads into a classical ceilidh routine, the opening dance sequence where we're all on stage.'

The outro finished on an exciting note, and Dair stood up and showed her a few of the opening moves based on ceilidh dancing.

She'd never seen anyone do a contra check like this in a ceilidh waltz.

'That's a powerful opening to the show,' she said, picturing the atmosphere.

Dair spoke as he danced around the floor. 'The routine is like a ceilidh with show dance elements. Not all the dances are Scottish,' he explained. 'There will be a variety of popular styles throughout the show — ballroom, Latin, everything from a tango to a cha–cha–cha. And Scottish Highland dancing as part of the choreography. I'm doing a Scottish sword dance.'

'And a Highland Fling?'

'Oh, yes,' he grinned and then stopped dancing. 'We don't have stage sets like your play. Everything will be created from the dancing, and the lighting.'

'Lighting is very effective. The dance show is reliant on the lighting effects to enhance the mood of the scenes.'

Dair hurried across to a table that he used for a desk where his laptop was set up. 'Come and have a look at the sketches for the costumes.'

Huntine went over and stood beside him while he showed her the sketches on screen.

'I love costume artwork,' she said. 'It's like fashion design illustrations.'

'We have a wonderful costume designer. All the costumes are vintage. Ball gowns, evening wear, everything has been worn for dancing in the past. Our designer calls them pre–loved. She's in the process of altering the designs to make them new for the show, while retaining a piece of their dancing past.'

'I like that idea.'

Dair was pleased that she approved. 'I'm even wearing a vintage kilt and ghillie shirt.'

'You're wearing a kilt?'

'For a couple of routines. Mainly, I'll wear the traditional, lace–up front ghillie shirts with trews.' He showed her a photo of himself in a dance pose while wearing a white ghillie shirt and dark trousers. The shirt's black laces were undone and showed his lean–muscled chest.

She recognised the picture from Dair's website promoting the dance show.

'The look suits you.'

'I think it'll work well for the show, and it feels great to wear for the dancing. But there are various costumes.' He showed her some of the other designs.

And then relented. 'Sorry, I'm taking up your time, when you're only here to discuss the lyrics.'

'It's all part of the show. The more I understand about your dance routines and themes, it'll help me write what you need.'

Those gorgeous eyes of his gazed down at her, and she wasn't sure what she sensed from him. But she knew her own reaction. Most women would find Dair attractive, and she found her heart fluttering unexpectedly, especially when he was standing so close to her.

'Tea?' he offered, blinking out of the moment.

'Tea would be great.'

'I'll put the kettle on.' He gestured around the room. 'Try your hand at playing guitar, tinkle the piano keys...'

Huntine smiled at him.

The last comment he cast back at her was the only one that sparked her real interest.

'Dance around the floor if you want. You've got it all to yourself.'

Oh, if only he knew how tempted she was. But the last thing she needed was to step back into her past, her dancing. It would only complicate everything.

Dair set the cups up while the kettle boiled, and chided himself. He was so tempted to invite Huntine to have dinner with him at one of his favourite restaurants in Edinburgh. A dinner date.

He fussed with the cups, mentally muttering that he would not do this. It would only spoil everything.

Huntine trailed her fingers so lightly over the piano keys that she didn't play a note. It was such a beautiful

35

piano, gleaming wood that reflected her uneasy expression in the highly polished lid. She sat down, wanting to feel what it would be like to play such a magnificent instrument, knowing she wouldn't.

So lost in thought, she jolted when Dair came through with the tea tray and sat it down on a table beside the couch.

'Don't get up,' he said, seeing her about to jump up from the piano stool.

'I was just admiring the craftsmanship of the piano.'

Dair was now standing next to her. 'Budge over.'

Without hardly giving her a moment to consider this, his body was now seated right beside her, and she could sense his eagerness to let her try her hand at playing a few notes.

'Place your hands like this.' He demonstrated and she was encouraged to follow his lead. 'Now press gently but firmly on the keys.'

An off–key note sounded from under her fingertips. She squirmed and lifted her hands off the keys immediately.

Dair stilled her hands, took charge and placed them on the keys again. This time, he kept his elegant fingers lightly touching hers, sending shivers of excitement through her.

She couldn't contain the blush forming across her cheeks, and she wasn't inclined to blush easily.

'Don't fret,' Dair advised in a calm voice, mistaking her blush for embarrassment. 'Breathe easy...and press down smoothly on the keys.'

The note sounded tuneful this time, and initiated a smiling reaction from her.

'It feels wonderful to play, doesn't it?' he said, looking at her in close–up with those eyes of his.

'It does. Though I think I'll stick to using a different type of keyboard, for my writing.'

'Come on, give it another go. Be a wee bit wild.'

'I can be wild, when the occasion merits it.' The comment was out before she could edit it.

'Then let's play together. Play the piano,' he corrected himself. 'What does Huntine Grey look like when she's a wee bit wild?'

Oh, if only he knew that too.

'I'll try for a few minutes, and then we really need to concentrate on the songs, the lyrics,' she insisted.

'Okay,' he said, and guided her hands on the keys. 'Try this. Feel the music at your fingertips.'

She did, and smiled at him.

After practising a few times, he let her play the notes on her own. 'Now, you play those, and I'll play a harmony. Ready?'

'Nope, but here goes...'

The melody they created was brief, but they were happy with their makeshift music.

Huntine sat upright and took her hands off the keys. 'That sounded okay, so I'm going to quit on a high note.'

Dair laughed and stood up. 'Let's drink our tea while it's still hot, then we'll work on the lyrics.'

She joined him at the table for tea.

He'd put a plate of shortbread petticoat tails on the tea tray. They both ate a piece while drinking their tea and discussing the songs.

Afterwards, Dair played the music on the piano and his guitar, while Huntine jotted down words for the lyrics.

He came and peered over her as she wrote them in her notebook.

'I like these. Are they a verse do you think? Or a chorus?'

'A chorus. These words would repeat quite well.' Then she looked at them again. 'Or they could be a refrain.'

'You really do know your lyric writing,' he remarked.

She looked up at him. 'I've always liked to write poetry, and I think of lyrics as musical poetry.'

Dair clasped the notebook and hurried over to the piano to try them.

'No, they're not finished. They need polished.'

He propped them up on the piano stand. 'They look sparkly enough to me.'

She shook her head at him and smiled, and then listened as he played and sang them.

When he finished, they looked at each other and nodded.

They continued to work together, each encouraging the other, until the afternoon light became a burnished amber glow.

'I'd better go,' she said, gathering her things. 'The afternoon has sparked in.'

Dair walked her out to her car. 'Thank you for coming over and helping to piece so much of the songs together with me. I appreciate you taking the time. Are you going home to work on your novel now?'

'No, I've a rehearsal night for the play at the studio.' She put her bag in the car and got ready to leave.

'I must read one of your romance novels,' he said.

'Are you into reading romance books?'

'I'd like to read one of yours. Can you recommend a title I should buy?'

Huntine reached over and took one of her paperbacks from the glove compartment and handed it to him. 'This is my latest book. A light–hearted romance set in Scotland.'

He smiled, delighted. 'Wait, you have to sign it for me.'

'No, Dair, you don't need me to do that.'

'I'd like you to sign it for me.' He patted his trouser pockets. 'I don't have a pen.' He grinned at her. 'Come on, you're a writer, you must have a zillion pens rattling around in your car.'

Huntine laughed as she took a pen from her bag, signed the title page of the book, and then added a personal message. Closing it, she handed the book back to him.

She waved as she drove off, and glanced in the mirror, seeing him open the book, read the message, and smile. *To Dair. I wish you all the best with your dancing and music. Huntine.*

Dair looked through the book as he went inside the house and closed the door. He sat down in the living room, intending to read the opening chapter, interested to see her writing style. Three chapters later, he put the book aside, having become engrossed in her story, surprised how much he was enjoying it.

Wandering through to the kitchen, he started to make himself dinner, and then work on his songs and choreography.

A twilight sky arched over the heart of Edinburgh as Huntine walked towards the dance studio. Energy was bubbling in the mild, spring evening as the city geared up for a night of fun and entertainment. Cafe bars and restaurants were brightly lit and buzzing with people enjoying dinner and a night out.

Lights shone from the entrance of the studio, and Huntine headed inside to the studio room where the play's cast and crew were preparing for another rehearsal.

As the lights dimmed for the opening of the play, she sat down next to Cambeul to watch the run through of Act One.

'Cutting it neat,' Cambeul whispered to her. 'I was about to phone you.'

'I've had a busy day writing,' she said, keeping her voice down.

'Song lyrics or your novel?'

'Both.'

'I hope you won't let Dair disrupt your book deadline.'

'I won't.'

'He's the sort of man to be a distraction. Especially when he has a proclivity to whip his shirt off.'

'Dair doesn't distract me. And he kept his shirt on today.'

'So you were with him?'

'We had a working lunch.'

'Where did he take you? Anywhere wonderful?'

'He cooked lunch at his house.'

Cambeul's script rustled as he fumbled with it.

'Then we worked all afternoon on the song lyrics. He played his piano and electric guitar. He's an excellent musician.'

'Is there anything he can't do?' Cambeul scoffed.

'Write.'

They were quiet for a few moments, and then Cambeul whispered to her. 'I'm not one for interfering, but I just don't want to see you become embroiled with a man who'll jeopardise your work. Especially as I've managed to line up a press interview.'

'Publicity for the play?'

'Yes, and they're keen to interview you about your playwriting.'

'When?'

'Tomorrow afternoon. I've arranged a meeting and afternoon tea. I hope you'll come along and chat to them.'

'Yes, I'm happy to do that, Cambeul.'

They settled down and watched the play unfold. Changes had been made to the script to add to the romantic drama.

At the end of the First Act, the lights were turned up and Cambeul and Huntine discussed the performance with the actors, with everyone agreeing that they liked the changes to the script.

After the rehearsal, Cambeul walked with Huntine to her car. His was parked nearby.

'The meeting for the interview is at three in the afternoon,' said Cambeul. 'I suggest we both arrive half an hour early to coordinate everything we'd like to chat about.

'I'll meet you there at two–thirty,' she agreed.

'He's a photo–journalist. He wants to do the interview first and then take some pics of us.'

'I'll wear something suitable,' she promised.

'You always dress well.'

'So do you, Cambeul. I don't think I've ever seen you do casual.'

He smiled, taking her compliment. 'Certainly never as casual as Dair. Though if the interview flatlines and we need to spark some interest, I might resort to his tactics and cast my shirt to the wind.'

'That's not a bad idea. Maybe I should make my interview replies boring so you can add some interesting drama.'

'I don't have a muscled physique like Dair, but I'm tall and lean enough to pass muster in the right light and a flattering angle.' He tapped his stomach. 'There's a three–pack in there somewhere.'

Huntine laughed as she got into her car. 'I'll see you tomorrow afternoon, Cambeul.'

She drove off through the heart of the city to her flat, thinking what a topsy–turvy day it had been. From being entertained by electric guitar music, and having her first, and probably last, piano lesson, to listening to her play's director devise a back–up plan to strip his shirt off.

Now her own plan was to work on her book, and write for a couple of hours before trying to get some sleep.

CHAPTER FOUR

Place your left hand on my shoulder
Clasp your other hand in mine
Let me lead you round the dance floor
Waltz with me in time...

Huntine closed her laptop, having worked on her book all morning from the cosy quietude of her flat. The living room window offered a view of the bustling city while the old–fashion structure and thickness of the walls created the hushed haven that she needed to write.

Breakfast was tea and toast, she'd worked right through lunch, and now it was time to get ready for the interview and afternoon tea.

Picking through her wardrobe, she realised she'd let her penchant for neutral tones almost exclude vibrant colours. Something to rectify she told herself, putting on a classy tea dress in shades of grey. Wearing her hair down, she added a touch more makeup for the photographs that were due to be taken. The mascara and silvery–grey shadow enhanced her eyes, but she kept her lipstick to her favourite soft rose.

Putting on her cream wool coat, she picked up her bag and headed out to arrive early as agreed.

Cambeul, wearing a classic suit, had just claimed their table in the elegant surroundings of the restaurant where they were having their meeting. All white linen, silver cake stands, dainty sandwiches, scones with cream and strawberry jam, and traditional cakes. The staff knew him and served up two cups of tea while they waited for the photo–journalist.

Huntine acknowledged that Cambeul was a good–looking man, but she felt no spark of attraction towards him. And although at times his comments jarred her, she'd become accustomed to having him in her life, and they worked well together even when at odds with what they wanted from the plays. The verbal tussles usually resulted in an elevated compromise, and the plays were all the better for it.

Dair had an afternoon meeting with his dance show's costume designer at their premises in Edinburgh.

All the costumes for Dair's show were vintage or pre–loved from stage performances and dance shows. The only items that were new were the professional dance shoes. These included ghillie brogues, designed for dancing.

He stepped out of the changing room wearing a redesigned ghillie shirt and snug–fitting, dark tartan trews.

The designer and her assistant fussed with his outfit, checking the fit of the shirt and the length of the trews. A type of trouser with tapered legs, a fishtail back and high, broad waistband. These had been worn as dancewear for a previous event, and were fashioned for flexibility.

'The fabric has a bit of movement in it,' the designer said to Dair.

He stretched his legs, trying the trews for comfort. 'I can move well in these. Nice fit.' The white cotton ghillie shirt was tucked into the waistband of the trews. Dair wore the laces at the neckline undone, the way he intended to wear it for dancing.

Various shirts and tailored trousers that had stretch in them hung on the rails, and were all included in his costume selection. One kilt dangled on a hanger.

Under the shop lights, the silk and satin shirts in jewel colours looked great.

He went behind the curtain and put on the rich ruby shirt he planned to wear for one of the dynamic numbers, perhaps the tango.

'Do you want me to add more sparkle?' the designer said to him.

'Yes, the sequin work on this jacket is exquisite.' Dair put the cropped jacket on. Black velvet glistened with beadwork. The silk lining felt wonderful against his bare skin.

'Try the other pairs of trousers on.'

Dair unhooked the items, took them into the changing room and hung them up. Then one by one he wore each pair, with next to no adjustments required.

'I think you've lost a bit of weight,' the designer assessed.

'A wee bit,' Dair agreed. 'The extra dancing, choreography, a busy schedule.' His muscles were even more defined.

'The ceilidh dresses, cocktail dresses and the ball gowns are ready,' the designer told him. 'Shona and the other ladies taking part in the show were in yesterday for their final fittings.' She gestured to the dresses hanging on rails, a mix of chiffon, silk, satin, including satin tartan. Fashioned with frills, fringing and frou–frou for the energetic numbers, to slinky, sensual styles, and fabulous ball gowns, the costumes filled the rails.

'Excellent work,' said Dair. 'I appreciate everything you've redesigned for the show.'

The designer lifted the chiffon hemline of a dress, seeing the floaty fabric glitter and the shine on a satin gown. 'I love seeing beautiful clothes taking another turn under the spotlights on stage rather than be discarded or left to languish in the back of a wardrobe.' She admired his kilt. 'I couldn't resist adding a sprinkling of sparkle to the plaid and the sporran. But I've sewn a fastening at the back of the sporran to keep it close to the kilt. You don't want it bouncing all over the place, even when you are.'

Dair had sent her a copy of the dancing from the rehearsals.

'I didn't know you could play the piano, the guitar and sing.' She sounded genuinely surprised. 'Performing your own songs too.'

'I have a wordsmith helping me write the lyrics,' he said, changing from one outfit to the other as she made tucks and notes for minor alterations.

'Oh, anyone I know?'

'Huntine Grey.' He doubted she'd know the name.

'The playwright?'

He was more surprised than her. 'Yes, she's working on a play at the moment. It's due to open this summer, around the same time as my show.'

'I've been working on the actors' costumes,' she revealed, sounding delighted. 'Cambeul hired me again. I've designed for his productions a few times.'

47

'What's he like?'

'Have you met him?' she said.

'I have, but...' he explained the shirtless circumstances. 'I get the impression he's set his cap at Huntine.'

She smiled. 'It's no secret. But according to the gossip, and you know there are no secrets in our world, Cambeul is waiting until she's mended her broken heart. He's giving her time, and then hoping to start dating her once the play is launched.'

'A broken heart?'

'You didn't know?'

Dair shook his head.

'Well...' She began to reveal the circumstances. 'I don't have the details, but the story goes that her boyfriend she thought was a steady, trustworthy sort, was cheating on her while they were dating. Apparently, he was a businessman, finance, accounts, not in our business, so she thought she'd picked a nice, reliable man.' She pinned one of the shirt sleeves to adjust the length. 'But he was a two–timing rotter.'

'When did they break up?'

'Fairly recent. That's why Cambeul is giving her time to unravel the web of lies her ex had spun around her. But everyone expects them to start dating. They spend a lot of time together and seem to get on.' She stepped back and checked the adjustments. 'I'll stitch these, and add more sparkle to a few things.'

'And can you give me any details about your next play?' the photo–journalist said to Huntine. He was recording the interview while they had afternoon tea and chatted about the forthcoming stage play.

'I have an idea in mind,' Huntine told him. 'It's another romantic drama. I'm still setting the stage for it, so to speak, creating the characters at the heart of the story.'

'Will it be set in modern–day Scotland?' said the photo–journalist.

'No, it'll be in the past,' Huntine explained.

'We're already thinking of it being another entertaining run in the theatres,' Cambeul chimed–in.

'Will you be collaborating on this together?' the photo–journalist wanted to clarify.

'Yes,' Huntine confirmed. 'Once I gauge the reaction to the new play, and finish my latest novel, I'll focus on the next play. But at the moment, we're busy with the current rehearsals.'

'Is your novel a romance?' said the photo–journalist. 'Are you on a deadline?'

'It's a contemporary romance,' she said. 'I have a deadline to finish it for my publishers. I'm working between the play's rehearsals and the novel.'

'And now writing song lyrics,' Cambeul added.

'For the play?' said the photo–journalist.

'No, for Dair's dance show.' She summarised the details.

The photo–journalist's interest increased. 'I didn't know you were a lyricist. Can you reveal any details about the songs and Dair's performance?'

'Details are on Dair's website,' she said. 'He'll be playing piano and guitar, and singing three of his own songs.'

'With your lyrics,' the photo–journalist remarked.

'Mainly mine, though Dair already had some of his own. We've reworked those too,' she said. 'You should talk to him. I'm sure he'd be happy to chat about his songwriting and his dancing.'

The photo–journalist nodded with enthusiasm. 'I'll do that.'

After the interview they went outside to have their photographs taken against the backdrop of the city. It was a bright, clear, afternoon, and the photo–journalist seemed to know what he wanted for the look of the feature.

'I'll let you know when this goes to press,' he said to Huntine and Cambeul, and then headed away while making a call to Dair.

Cambeul rubbed his hands together. 'I think that went well.'

'It did, though I didn't expect you to mention the lyrics.'

'Sorry, it just popped out. But it'll add interest to the feature.'

Huntine took her phone out. 'I'd better call Dair and tell him what's happened.' His phone was busy, so she left a message.

Dair was still wearing one of the ghillie shirts while taking a face–to–face call from the photo–journalist.

'I'm finishing having a costume fitting,' said Dair, explaining his stylish look, and revealing that the clothes were pre–loved.

The photo–journalist told him about the interview he'd just had with Huntine and Cambeul, and wanted to interview Dair for an accompanying feature that was due to be published in the newspaper's magazine supplement.

They agreed to meet at a nearby eatery within the next half hour.

Dair changed out of his costume trousers, but kept the white ghillie shirt on, suitably laced up. He made a quick call to Huntine.

'Where are you?'

Huntine told him. 'I left a message—'

'I got it, but the photo–journalist called me and he wants to interview us in an eatery he knows that has a piano customers can play. Can you join me? Are you still nearby?'

'I am. I can be there in a few minutes,' she said.

'It's a great opportunity for publicity for both of us.' Dair was already heading out into the city and making his way to the eatery. 'The photo–journalist says he has a deadline for the supplement's features, and he wants to fit this one in too.'

'I'll meet you there soon.'

The call ended on an exciting note.

Dair was seated at the piano and talking to the photo–journalist when Huntine arrived. They'd ordered tea.

'Thanks for coming along,' the photo–journalist said to her. 'While it's fairly quiet in here, can I get a few pictures of the two of you with the piano?'

Huntine took her coat off and stood beside the piano while Dair sat with his hands on the keys.

'Stand a bit closer to the piano, Huntine. That's great. Dair, look like you're playing the piano and now...smile.'

Several pictures were taken and the photo–journalist checked the previews and seemed happy with them.

'I'm thinking of a heading like — *Dairing Dancer in tune with Romance Writer.*'

Dair and Huntine glanced at each other, happy with the headline.

'So tell me about your songwriting and lyrics within that sort of theme.' The photo–journalist began recording the interview.

'I needed help with my song lyrics,' Dair explained. 'I met Huntine at the dance studio during both our shows' rehearsals. I found out she was a writer, and she's kindly agreed to write lyrics for my new songs that I'll perform on the tour.'

'Will you be singing or playing at any of Dair's shows?' the photo–journalist said to her.

Huntine blinked. 'No, I don't play piano or guitar, or sing.'

'Do you dance?' the photo–journalist added. 'Are you dancing with Dair during the tour?'

Huntine side–stepped the first part of the question and replied to the latter part. 'I won't be dancing. I'm just the lyric writer.'

Gleaning everything he needed for the editorial, the photo–journalist stood up. 'These two features could make the paper's online edition tomorrow, and then be published in the magazine supplement a few days later. I'll let you know.' Smiling, he then left to get the features written.

Dair started playing the piano. Customers were encouraged to play, and Huntine relaxed for a few moments listening to him. But her eyes were drawn to his ghillie shirt.

'I was at a costume fitting,' he explained, seeing her glance at him. 'I decided to keep the shirt on for the photos.'

'You suit it,' she said.

As the interview was over, she went to put on her coat to leave.

'Do you want to have something to eat while we're here?' he offered. 'An early dinner.'

'It would save me from rustling up dinner when I get back to my flat,' she reasoned. 'I was so busy during my interview earlier with Cambeul, that I didn't eat much from the afternoon tea.'

They sat at a table for two beside the piano.

Dair read the menu. 'I quite fancy the breaded fish with chunky chips, peas and salad.'

'That sounds tasty.' Huntine closed her menu.

While they waited on their order being served, they spoke about the lyrics, and Dair sidled on to the piano stool beside their table and played a verse and chorus of one of the new songs.

The handful of other diners smiled over at him, listening and enjoying his piano playing.

Dair stopped when their meal was served, and they continued chatting over dinner.

'I've been reading your book, and enjoying it,' he said. 'I intend to finish it. I like your writing.'

'I'm pleased you're enjoying the book.'

'And I'm really happy with the song lyrics you're writing for me,' he said.

'Are you going to record your songs professionally?'

'I hadn't considered that.'

'Maybe you should. If you had them recorded in a music studio, you could offer them as digital downloads from your website.'

Dair looked interested. 'You mentioned to me that you worked with recording studios.'

'Yes. You could book a recording session at a music studio once you're happy with the three songs. Find one that has a piano you can hire to play, and take your guitars with you, or your keyboard. And confirm that they offer a sound engineer, and mixing and mastering services. Maybe talk this over with your dance tour director.'

A wave of excitement charged through him. 'I'll do that.'

They discussed this further while finishing their meal.

Afterwards, Dair walked Huntine to her car. They enjoyed the early evening stroll through the city.

The spring air had a mild crispness to it that refreshed their senses after such an intense day of interviews and then making plans for the music recordings.

'I'm grateful for your ideas,' he said. 'You've given me so much to think about and plan.'

'I have a tendency to meddle.'

'Meddle all you want.'

She smiled at him.

'I mean it,' he insisted. 'What other meddling do you have in mind? Other suggestions.'

'I really don't want to interfere with your dance tour but...'

He urged her to reveal her thoughts.

'Have you considered filming your show so that people who missed seeing it live in the theatres can watch it after the tour is finished?'

Her suggestion jolted Dair. 'Film the dance show! No, I hadn't.' He sounded excited about this.

Huntine discussed her idea. 'Hire a video production team. One that uses multiple cameras for the full stage setting. Wide, medium and close–up shots to showcase all the dancers and their skills. Audio quality is important. Check they handle the post–production too. The editing of the raw footage.'

'You sound as if you have experience of this as well.'

'I grew up around the theatre, shows, plays, musical performances,' she said. 'With the technical equipment and services available these days, it's entirely feasible. Lots of events are filmed and sold to extend the audience views.'

Dair nodded as she spoke, picturing that he'd love to do this. 'Would they film the opening night? Or would it be better to video one of the other shows further into the tour?'

'I was thinking more along the lines of filming a full dress rehearsal. No audience. Then if something goes awry, you can run through that part of the routine again.'

Dair stopped and gazed at her. 'Why didn't I think of doing this?'

'It's your first tour, and you're concentrating on the choreography, and the songs. Sometimes it takes an outsider to poke their nose in. As I say, I've a tendency to meddle. But whether it's dancing on stage, singing and playing, or writing books and plays, it's all entertainment. That's how I look on it.' Then she added another suggestion. 'You could hire the stage room at the studio for the filming. It would have the feeling of a real stage setting, and you're familiar with the facilities.'

'Is your new play going to be recorded?'

'I'm discussing this with Cambeul. We almost did it for the last play we worked on. He's talking to a video production team about the choice of format. There are discs, and different types of downloads that would be available from the play's website under Cambeul's management. He says USB memory sticks are popular for people to buy with the recording on it. They can then watch it on various devices.'

Dair's mind whirred with excitement, and he was eager to discuss this too with his tour director.

'It would be a wonderful way to connect with a wider audience,' said Dair.

They walked to where magnificent Edinburgh castle glowed against the sky.

'I love meandering through the city at night,' she said. 'The historic grandeur is quite breathtaking.'

Dair agreed, and then added a comment about her book. 'I like the Scottish Highlands setting of your novel. The laird and the castle. Not a crumbling castle.'

'Nooo. The castle and characters are pure fiction. But the lairds I've known all lived in beautiful, well–maintained castles.'

'Reading about it makes me want to tour the Highlands,' he said. 'Though I'm looking forward to a few of the dance tour venues being in cities and towns up north. And performing on one of the islands.'

'It sounds such an exciting tour.'

'Yes,' he agreed, and continued to walk with her to her car where he bid her goodnight. 'Hopefully, the interviews will be published in the paper's online edition tomorrow.'

'It'll be interesting to see if the sub–editor includes the Dairing Dancer headline.'

Dair smiled at her. 'In tune with the romance writer.'

Huntine got into her car and he waved her off, then walked on to where his car was parked.

The sky looked like a deep blue watercolour awash with bands of deep pink and lilac. The buzz of the vibrant city hummed in the background.

Unable to contain his eagerness to discuss the recording plans, Dair phoned his tour director, who had a network of connections in the industry, and chatted as he walked along.

'I know a few people in the music recording and video film business. I like Huntine's ideas. I'll make some calls to them and get back to you. And I'll phone the dance studio and make a provisional booking for the stage room. See what dates they have available.

It'll be handy anyway for a full dress rehearsal of the show on a stage setting.'

'Yes, make the booking now,' Dair advised. 'The studio has been busy lately.'

'I'll phone them right now and call you back.'

Dair put his phone in his pocket and breathed in the energy of the night. He was still wearing the ghillie shirt, but it somehow made him feel part of the Scottish city's traditional past, while not looking too out of place. Walking across an area where there were trees and greenery, he saw some couples strolling along, arm in arm, or holding hands. And in that moment, he felt the urge to find such happiness and romance with the woman one day meant for him.

CHAPTER FIVE

Play piano, play guitar
Sing the words of our song
Play guitar, play piano
Stay with me where you belong...

'I've booked the stage room one evening about a week before the dance tour kicks off,' the tour director told Dair, phoning him later that night.

Dair took a note of the date and time.

'And I'm going to call a few people about the recordings for the songs and the video.'

'Thanks,' said Dair. 'Let me know what they say.'

'I will.'

Dair finished the call on a hopeful note, and proceeded to practise the dance choreography in his living room. He was working on a few new moves for Act Two. But his mind was whirring with ideas for both of the recordings, and he turned the music up in an effort to drown this out so he could concentrate on the choreography.

Huntine's fingers tapped quickly on the keys of her laptop as she sat in her flat working on her book. It was late at night, and the shimmering lights of Edinburgh provided a romantic view of the beautiful city from her window.

Steeped in her story, deep in another chapter, she pushed thoughts of Dair to the margins not wanting to be distracted.

Finally, she closed her laptop and got ready for bed, making herself a cup of tea and mulling over the meddling she'd caused. She'd sparked ideas in Dair.

Sipping her tea, she stood at her bedroom window that offered another light show of the city. She did love Edinburgh, but she would be going home to Glasgow in the not too distant future. Dair would be part of her past.

Images of him wearing that ghillie shirt and looking so handsome flickered through her mind. Sighing to herself, she climbed into bed, pushing these thoughts aside, for no happy ending could ever come from letting her guard down and becoming romantically involved with Dair. He was a temptation, and in a sense she was relieved that her broken heart showed signs of mending. And this was all the more reason why she didn't want another dose of heartbreak.

Huntine popped to the niche of little shops near her flat the following morning to buy fresh bread, cheese and milk. As she came out of the grocery shop, she noticed a dress in the window of the pretty vintage clothes shop.

She stood for a moment admiring the lovely turquoise tea dress. A wrap style suitable for wearing during the day or evening. It reminded her of the colour of the turquoise sea in the Highlands, and she went inside the shop to try it on. Being a wrap dress, it could be adjusted to fit her well. It skimmed mid–calf, and the fabric was a soft cotton.

'It's a lovely colour on you,' the shop assistant said as Huntine looked at herself in the mirror. A few customers were in picking up a bargain from the new stock that had just arrived.

'I'll take it,' Huntine decided.

Paying for the dress, she stepped out into the morning sunlight, and as she was walking back to her flat, Dair phoned.

'The photo–journalist called me. The interviews are published on the paper's online edition this morning. And they'll be in the magazine supplement in a couple of days.'

'I'll check out the website. I'm on my way back to my flat.'

'The features and the photos look great!' Dair enthused. 'Take a look, and call me back to let me know what you think.'

'I'll do that.'

Huntine hurried back to her flat to read the features.

She read what was written, delighted with the editorials, and then studied the photographs. Her heart reacted seeing herself standing beside Dair as he sat at the piano. The pictures from the earlier interview with Cambeul in the frame were great too, but her attention kept being drawn to the photos with Dair. Their smiles portrayed their joy of being together, and surprised her how much they looked like a well–matched couple. Unlike the ones when she was with Cambeul. There was a theatrical, but businesslike vibe to them. Accurate, she assessed. So did that mean the impression of closeness with Dair was equally reliable?

She was so steeped in her own, deep thoughts that Dair's call jarred her.

Impatient to know what she thought, he'd called her. 'Well, thumbs up, down or sideways?'

'Thumbs up, all round. The editorials and the pictures are wonderful.'

Dair's grin widened as he smiled out the phone. 'I've called the photo–journalist and thanked him. But we have to do something to celebrate.' An idea sprang to mind. 'Come over for lunch.'

'To your house?' she clarified.

'Yes, I'll rustle up something tasty.'

'Again.'

'An encore lunch. With extra tea. Maybe even pudding.'

'I'm sold.'

Dair laughed. 'Come over when you're ready.'

Huntine clicked the phone off and eyed the vintage clothes shop bag. Peering in at the turquoise bargain buy, she decided to give the dress its first outing.

Refreshing her makeup, and brushing her blonde hair, she put the dress on and stepped into a pair of her favourite shoes. Dance shoes, a nice neutral tone classic court, disguised as regular shoes, but designed for dancing comfort. Like most of her shoes. For daytime and business, casual or evening wear, she bought her shoes from ranges designed for dancing. The colours and styles were lovely, from mid–heel courts to pretty pumps, in champagne to classic black, gold and silver. And they were comfortable. She could dance in them too, if she had the notion, and she still did sometimes, even though dancing wasn't part of her world now.

Huntine arrived at Dair's house for lunch, and like before, he didn't hear her when she knocked on the front door, so she went round the back to the kitchen.

Peering through the window, she saw him busily preparing the lunch. The kitchen cabaret was in full swing, and she stood for a moment enjoying his entertaining moves that included a shimmy across the kitchen to check on whatever was cooking in the oven. Clearly happy with it, he then whirred the tea towel above his head. Hopefully in a gesture of triumph, and not because he was wafting away the fumes.

Music played in the background, and she recognised the song as one of his own recordings. He proceeded to try out choreography moves he'd been working on. Clearly, he was wearing dancer's trousers with a lot of stretch in the fabric as he did a slow and controlled kick high above his head. A finale move, she assumed, as he then began setting up the plates and cutlery on the kitchen table.

Huntine knocked on the door and opened it.

'Perfect timing.' He grabbed the mitts and lifted a tray of sizzling fish in crispy breadcrumbs from the oven.

'Want a hand to make the tea?' she offered as the kettle clicked off the boil.

'That would be great.' He served up two pieces of fish on to their plates. Putting the tray back in the oven, he drained a pot of Ayrshire potatoes and added them to the plates, along with peas and a garnish of salad.

Huntine put two mugs of tea on the table.

They manoeuvred around each other as if their kitchen choreography had been rehearsed.

'You look lovely in that dress,' he said, reaching over and turning the music off so they could chat quietly over lunch.

'An impulse buy from a vintage clothes shop this morning. I only popped out for fresh bread, cheddar and milk. The colour caught my eye.'

'You certainly catch mine when you're wearing it.'

Huntine paused from adding the jar of pickle to the table.

Realising he'd revealed too much, he rewound his comment. 'What I mean is, you suit that colour. I don't think I've seen you wearing anything so vibrant.'

'I need to jazz up my neutral wardrobe.'

'You look lovely in your classy greys and whites. But a dash of colour would be fun too. Especially if I'm going to encourage you to be a wee bit wild.'

She smiled and sat down at the table. 'You're determined to be a bad influence on me.'

He sat down opposite her and gestured to her dress. 'You're wearing dazzling turquoise, and having lunch with me again. I think I've made huge progress already.'

She laughed.

'You should probably be ensconced in your writing garret, grabbing a cheese sandwich for lunch, while working on chapter someteenth.'

'Time out for bad behaviour to celebrate the features.'

'I'll drink to that.' Dair lifted his mug of tea.

She tipped hers against his. 'Cheers!'

'Cheers!'

'This is tasty,' she said, enjoying her meal.

'I thought it was a safe bet that you'd like fish and tatties as you liked your fish and chips dinner yesterday,' he reasoned.

She nodded. 'I told Cambeul that the features are on the website. He's delighted, and thinks it's great publicity.'

'It is,' Dair agreed. 'Excellent write–ups. And the pictures are wonderful. I particularly like the one of us. You look happy to be with me.' He narrowed his eyes jokingly. 'Are you sure you're not secretly a thespian?'

'I don't act. I don't sing.' She cut into the crisp breadcrumbs and continued to eat her lunch.

'Do you dance?'

Her grey eyes glanced over at him.

He mistook her hesitation for a lack of skill. 'I'd be happy to teach you,' he offered. 'Dance lessons thrown in while we work on the songs. We'd start with a traditional ballroom waltz. And work our way up to a tango.'

Huntine let him ramble on, hoping he'd run out of steam.

'You'd need a red dress for our tantalising tango,' he continued. 'But by that time you'll have gravitated out of the pastels and into the scorching scarlet tones.'

When her phone rang and she saw that the caller was her grandmother, Huntine smiled with relief, rescued from the conversation about dancing.

'It's my gran, calling from Glasgow,' she said to Dair. 'Do you mind if I take it?'

'Not at all.' Sitting back, he tucked into his food while she spoke to her grandmother. They had a face–to–face call on speaker.

Her grandmother's cheery face beamed out at her. In her retirement years, she was pretty and wore her silvery–blonde hair swept up in a soft bun.

'I see you're featured in the newspaper!' her gran said excitedly. 'On their website. Your grandfather always checks the daily news. You can imagine the surprise we got when we saw you in two stories. One with Cambeul. And one with that gorgeous dancer, Dair. You've been keeping him a secret. What a dancer he is! We saw him perform last year in a show in Glasgow. And sooo handsome. No wonder you're smiling, Huntine.'

Dair had a mouthful of food, but his shoulders shook trying to contain his laughter.

'I was going to tell you once the features were published in the paper's magazine,' Huntine managed to say, before her grandmother's enthusiasm took over the conversation.

'He's single, or so I've read. Are you having a wee romance while you're over there in Edinburgh? You've never fancied Cambeul. But I wouldn't blame you enjoying a fling with a handsome dancer like Dair.'

'No! Nothing like that, we're—'

'Congratulations, Huntine!' Her grandfather's smiling face appeared behind his wife. 'And I see you're back to writing song lyrics.'

'Yes, as it says in the feature, I'm helping to write the lyrics for Dair's new songs.'

Her grandmother took over the conversation again. 'Are you dancing with Dair during his tour?'

'No.' Huntine tried to dowse the topic.

'Why not?' Her grandmother frowned. 'The two of you would light up the stage with your dancing.'

By now, Dair had put his cutlery down and was blinking, wondering if he was picking up what was being said.

'No,' Huntine's one–word reply aimed to stop the topic again. And failed.

'Oh, the pair of you would've shone like stars. And he's such a looker.'

'Gran, Dair's here right now,' Huntine cut–in. 'We're having lunch.' Huntine turned the phone around to show Dair's surprised but smiling face.

'Pleased to meet you,' said Dair. 'And you too,' he added to her grandfather.

'Och! You should've told me, Huntine. And not let me open my mouth and let my gums rattle.'

Dair laughed.

'Ach, well.' Her grandmother adjusted her shoulders and tried not to squirm with embarrassment. 'We're both delighted for the two of you, and Cambeul of course, being featured in the news.'

'What theatre was it that you saw me perform?' Dair said to Huntine's grandparents.

'The theatre I used to manage before I retired a few years ago,' her grandfather said to Dair. He named the theatre in Glasgow. 'I'm Jock by the way. And this is my wife, Jessy. She was, and still is, a wonderful dancer — ballet, ballroom, stage dancing. We met when she was the lead dancer in a show at the theatre. That's where Huntine got her dancing talent. Jessy taught her ballet, and she learned ballroom and stage dancing. A shining talent when she was a wee girl and a young woman, but her writing eventually outshone everything.'

Huntine hoped that Dair wouldn't cause ripples and that she could explain to him later that she could dance. Unfortunately, Dair was in the opposite frame of mind.

'I didn't know Huntine could dance,' Dair told them.

Jock and Jessy exchanged a look of disbelief. And then Jessy threw a blunt question at her granddaughter. 'Why did you keep your dancing a secret from Dair?'

Three faces stared at Huntine, waiting for an answer.

Lie, truth or tell Dair later? Huntine's options juggled for top position.

'I'm concentrating on my writing,' said Huntine. 'I don't want anything else to muddle my schedule.'

Her grandparents were so enthralled with the features to need further explanation, though Dair looked like he had a ton of questions piling up and waiting for her once the call was finished.

'I'll organise tickets for you to come to any of the shows when my tour is in Glasgow,' Dair said to her grandparents.

Their faces lit up. 'Oh, that would be marvellous,' said Jessy.

'Yes, we'd love to go,' Jock added.

'I'll coordinate the dates and times for you with Huntine,' said Dair. 'The tickets will be the meet and greet ones, so please do come backstage after the show and say hello.'

'We'll do that,' Jessy said, smiling brightly.

Waving, her grandparents finished the call, leaving Huntine facing Dair.

'Ballet, ballroom and stage dancing.' He picked up his cutlery and finished his potatoes.

Huntine smiled tightly. 'Surprise!'

'Any other hidden talents I should know about? Tap? Highland dancing? Ceilidh dancing?'

'Not tap.'

Her reply took him aback again. He leaned forward, and those blue eyes of his locked with hers. 'Anything else?'

'No...well, unless you include baton twirling. I was a wee majorette.'

A smile formed on his sensual lips. 'So, you're a Highland dancing, baton twirling, ceilidh skirling, stage performing, ballroom dancing ballerina.'

'Pretty much. Or I used to be.'

'And a wee scallywag for not telling me.'

'That too,' she admitted playfully. 'But I hung up my dancing shoes a while ago.'

69

Dair peered down at her feet under the table. 'Those look suspiciously like ballroom dance shoes.'

'They are, but I only wear them because they're stylish, look like ordinary shoes, and they're comfy.'

Dair stood up, cast his napkin down on the table, clasped her hand and pulled her up.

'There's a forfeit to pay for being a sneaky scallywag.' He pulled her through to the living room.

Huntine giggled as he flicked the music on, and led her on to the middle of the floor, without letting go of her hand.

'Do you think I'm going to make a run for it?' she teased him.

'I wouldn't put anything past you now.' He gave her a challenging look. 'Name your dance.'

She listened to the music and then decided. 'Slow foxtrot.'

'Nice,' he agreed, nodding. 'One of my favourites.'

Taking her in hold, they began to foxtrot across the diagonal of the floor.

Her feather steps, promenade pivots and smooth, gliding movements were in perfect time with his.

'Let's waltz,' said Dair after a few minutes.

Huntine waltzed around the floor with Dair. A traditional waltz.

As the song finished, they ended the dance in close hold. Their lips were a breath apart, and he looked at her longingly, as if he wanted to kiss her, but then he pulled back and released her from arms.

'You're a lovely dancer, Huntine,' he said, brushing a hand through his hair to clear the tempting, sensual thoughts from his mind.

'I loved my dancing,' she said. 'I still do. But I chose to be a writer. I tried to do both, but as you know, dancing to a high, professional standard takes hours of regular dedication and hard training. And writing plays and books requires even more time. I couldn't do both without them becoming less than they might have been.'

'I understand, truly. Though I wish I'd known you could dance.'

'I've been lied to and cheated romantically in the past few years,' she confessed. 'I dated a dancer. I thought we were a happy couple. But he was secretly in love with another ballerina. So, once I'd mended that broken heart, I ventured into the dating arena again, thinking that a man outwith the dancing and entertainment business would be a safer choice. An accountant, working in finance. But, lightning struck me in the same place twice, and so here I am in Edinburgh, still reeling from the latest broken heart. My defences are still up. Not just for romance. But in general. I'm concentrating on my play and my novel. I'm happy with those. And writing a few song lyrics. If I seem guarded, it's because I am.'

Dair nodded, and they started to walk through to the kitchen. 'Tea?' he offered lightly, bringing the conversation back to a safer topic.

Huntine halted and glared at him. 'I was promised pudding.'

'Indeed you were. How does chocolate chip ice cream sound?'

'Perfect.'

Dair cleared the main course dishes away and served up two generous scoops of ice cream. 'With or without a skoosh of whipped cream?'

'With. We're celebrating.'

Sitting down at the table again, they ate their pudding.

'The Glasgow dates for the shows are on the website,' he said. 'Find out what night suits your grandparents so that I can arrange their tickets. Some theatres have sold most of the tickets already.'

'I'll phone them soon. And thank you for inviting them. They love dancing and the theatre. Although my grandfather retired as a theatre manager, he's still involved in the theatre circuit. So if you need information on any other venues, contact him.'

'I'll do that. My tour director wants to add more venues around Glasgow and the west coast, so I'll put him in touch with Jock.'

Huntine smiled brightly.

'I also plan to invite a few members of the audience at each show up on to the stage for a wee dance. Would your grandmother be up for that?'

Huntine's smiled brightened even more. 'She'd love to dance with you on stage. Even for a few moments. And she's a wonderful dancer.'

'Make a booking for your gran to dance with me.'

Huntine was so delighted for her grandparents, knowing how much they'd enjoy seeing the show, and taking part, that she scooped up a large spoonful of ice cream and didn't know that her nose was tipped with whipped cream.

Dair pondered for a moment, watching her happily eat her pudding, unaware that she had cream on her nose. Then he smiled and reached forward gently, and wiped it off.

The gesture, the gentleness, the intimacy of him doing this, sent shivers of excitement through her, and she blushed. Not from embarrassment that she'd splodged cream on her nose, but from Dair and the feelings he ignited in her.

CHAPTER SIX

Tango, and dance with me tonight
Under the sparkling ballroom light
It's the perfect night for us to shine
I feel that you are truly mine
If only for this dance
Tango with me tonight...

'I have some more lyrics for you,' Huntine said to Dair as they went through to the living room after lunch.

'Great.'

'I'll get my laptop. It's in the car.'

While Huntine went out to get her laptop, Dair sat down at his piano and began to play part of one of the songs he was working on.

Huntine came back in, accessed the lyrics on her laptop and commented on the tune Dair was playing.

'That sounds lovely. Is it a new piece?'

'It's a variation of one of the songs for the show. Your lyrics have helped me to come up with better versions of the original tunes.' He stopped playing and came over and sat beside her on the couch to read the lyrics on the laptop.

'I was writing my book, and then these lyrics popped into my head, and I wrote them down. I don't have them on paper.'

'That's fine.' He seemed engrossed in the words.

'These feel like verses for your second song,' she said. 'Though maybe they don't fit.'

Dair shook his head. 'No, my original lyrics need upgraded. These are far more romantic.'

'Too romantic?' She looked at him, as they sat close together.

'There's never too much romance in my world. Especially for the songs, the performance for the show.' He ran a frustrated hand through his hair. 'I can dance the romance I feel for the song, but I can't express it enough in words.' He sighed heavily. 'So, it's over to you, wordsmith.'

Huntine sat back on the couch with her laptop, ready to write anything that sprang to mind. 'Dance, Dair.'

'Okay.' He stood up and walked to the middle of the floor. Taking a moment to hear the music in his head, he began to dance, strong, elegant moves, expressing what he felt. Love, hope, heartache, fighting for the woman he loved, showing her how he felt...

The silence was exactly what Huntine needed. She wrote her plays and books in silence. No background music, no ambiance of a coffee shop, nothing like that. Other sounds interrupted the dialogue of her characters, the narrative of her stories. At home in Glasgow, she worked for hours on end in the quietude, resulting in writing scenes for her plays, and chapters for her books, uninterrupted by other words filtering into her thoughts.

The only sounds were Dair's light footsteps as he danced across the floor. Like Huntine, he was wearing dance shoes, a habit he'd attained, especially when he was at home, for he often thought of dance moves and would perform them in the living room. Spur of the moment bolts of inspiration. So he tended to wear his dance shoes, preferring the comfort and the flexibility.

Dair's footsteps beat out a rhythm, intertwined by the grand gestures, jumps and extensions.

Huntine watched every move, feeling she'd long remember these special moments when she was Dair's audience of one. The first to experience his mastery of dance and skill for the new choreography. The power emanating from him set her heart alight. And without a single note of music. The purest essence of his dancing.

The words started to flicker through her...a few at first, and then a floodgate of lyrics made her type at speed to capture them before they quickly disappeared to be replaced by the next line of lyrics.

Able to touch type, Huntine watched him while she typed the lyrics, and she could see him smile, knowing he'd once again tapped into the wordsmith in her through his dancing.

Jotting down notes with paper and pen was handy, but it required her to look at the paper. This way was faster and enabled her to watch his choreography while she wrote the words.

So in sync, they finished naturally together. The air was charged with the energy from the dancing and the writing. Both of them sensed that something special had just been created. Something that audiences would see in the not too distant future at the show.

Dair walked over and sat down, barely out of breath.

'Can I read what you've written?'

Huntine showed him the lyrics.

She watched his clear blue eyes read the verses, and saw him smile as he enjoyed what she'd come up with.

He was so handsome in profile, she thought, and then scolded herself for letting her thoughts drift, and gave her full focus to the work.

'I love these romantic lyrics,' he enthused.

'I loved your choreography.'

'Hopefully, combined, we've got something workable for the show.'

She sent him a copy of the lyrics, and he printed them out.

Setting the printout on the piano stand, he sat down and began to play the latest variation of the song, with the new lyrics.

Huntine knew she was listening to something special, memorable. And very romantic.

As he finished playing, a call came through for her, and she looked surprised when she saw who it was.

'Something wrong?' said Dair.

'It's the radio. The Mullcairn show,' she said, taking the call on speaker.

Dair knew the popular show and often listened in. Mullcairn was the radio presenter, a cheery man in his fifties, with a love of music, the theatre and lively chatter. Dair had never been a guest on the show, but Huntine had.

'Hello, Huntine, I'm Mullcairn's assistant. He read your press features today and is interested in chatting to you about your new play, latest novel — and your lyric writing.' she said. 'It's short notice, but he wondered if you'd like to pop along to the studio in Edinburgh this evening to be his guest tonight.'

Huntine didn't hesitate. She'd enjoyed herself the last two times she'd been on his show over the past two years. 'Yes, I'm in Edinburgh, so I could come along this evening.'

'Wonderful, Huntine. The show starts at seven, but pop along about six–thirty for a wee off–air chat. It'll be a live interview, as before, and Mullcairn will want to talk to you about what he plans to discuss.'

'I'll be there early,' Huntine confirmed.

'Mullcairn has spoken to you before about your plays and your romance novels, but your song lyrics are something new, so he'd like to include a chat about writing lyrics for Dair the dancer.'

'I'd be happy to talk about the lyrics. I'm actually here with Dair right now, working on his new lyrics for his dance show.'

'Could you hang on a wee minute, Huntine.' The line went on hold.

Huntine shrugged at Dair. 'I'm guessing she's telling Mullcairn about this and probably—'

'Hello, Huntine — and Dair, if you can hear me. I've just told Mullcairn what you're up to. Is there any chance that you could bring Dair with you tonight? Mullcairn would love to have him as a guest on the show too.'

He gave Huntine the thumbs up.

'Dair would be delighted to be a guest. We'll both be there tonight.'

'Marvellous. We'll see the pair of you this evening. And remember, it's a live show, so explain to

Dair that he has to watch his tongue. As a rule of thumb, he can use words like bahookie, sparingly, but we draw the line at bawbags.'

'I'll tell Dair,' Huntine assured her.

Dair pressed his lips together to stifle a guffaw, and let it go when the call finished.

'You can't do that!' Huntine scolded him. 'Mullcairn's show is lively, fun, and there will be moments when you'll have to button your lips.'

'I will. I promise. And I love the show.'

'So you're familiar with Mullcairn's cheery and chirpy style of presenting.'

'I am. But I've never been on the radio before.'

'You'll enjoy it. Just behave yourself, okay?'

'Okay.'

Huntine took a deep breath and checked the time. 'I suppose I'd better get home, and then come back here so we can go to the studio together. Or I'll meet you there.'

'That makes no sense. Stay here. We'll work on the songs. Then I'll drive us up to the studio. We can figure out dinner in the whirlwind.'

'That sounds like a plan.'

'Tea?' he offered.

'I'll make it. You keep singing and playing.'

Leaving Dair to practise at the piano, Huntine went through to the kitchen, made the tea, and brought it into the living room.

She sat the tea tray down on the table beside the couch. 'Two pieces of shortbread jumped on to a plate, so...'

Dair smiled, stopped playing, and came over to help himself to the tea and shortbread. 'Fuel for tonight.'

'Exactly.' Huntine lifted up the other piece and took a bite of the delicious all–butter shortbread.

Dair sipped his tea and they relaxed on the couch.

'I'll send a message to Cambeul and tell him to listen to the show,' said Huntine.

'Will he be miffed that he's not invited?'

'Nooo, he passed up the chance twice before. He gets jittery at the thought of being interviewed live in case he freezes or fumbles and says something inappropriate.'

'Like bawbags.'

Huntine laughed and sent the message to Cambeul. Moments later, she received a reply. 'Cambeul will be listening in and wishes us a great night.' Then she sent a quick message to her grandparents. 'They'll want to listen in.'

Putting her phone aside, she ate her shortbread and drank her tea. Her attention was drawn to the garden. 'It looks like a lovely bright afternoon. You're lucky to have a nice garden to step out on to.'

'Slurp down the rest of your tea, and we'll go for a meander round the garden. Get some fresh air.'

Huntine brightened at the idea.

Dair opened the patio doors and they stepped out into the mild afternoon air. Sunlight shone in the pale blue sky, and the spring flowers added splashes of yellow, blue, white, and lilac to the greenery.

They walked side by side across the lawn into the full glow of the sunshine, and Huntine breathed in the calm, fragrant air. 'This is nice.'

'Simple pleasures are always the best,' he said, easing any tension from his shoulders.

'True.' Huntine gazed up at the sky and felt the mild warmth of the sun on her face. 'You really are a bad influence on me. I should be in my flat, my garret, writing chapter someteenth.'

Dair smiled. 'I was thinking of taking advantage of you this afternoon. There's time before we need to get ready for the radio show.'

Huntine glanced at him.

'Would you give me your opinion, as a dancer, on my choreography?' he clarified.

'Yes, but you're the expert.'

'I'd value your thoughts, especially on the new routine I showed you.'

'Okay.'

They went back inside the living room, and Dair danced while Huntine sat on the couch watching him.

'This routine is a key part of the show,' he said. 'For the opening, I'll sing and play one of my songs on the piano, and then launch into the dance number.' He proceeded to show her the moves. 'You've seen part of this before, but I've changed the sequence to include more drama in the routine.'

He finished, and then wanted her thoughts on it.

'I think it's a powerful piece. The lighting will play an important role in creating the mood, and I'm picturing the atmosphere of this on stage. I really don't

81

want to mess with your routine, or meddle with your choreography.'

'Please, meddle.'

Huntine stood up and went over to where he was standing near the middle of the floor. 'Where's the audience? The front of stage?'

Dair opened his arms and gestured to it. 'The audience is there. This is stage right, and stage left.'

'The thing I notice is, you give more attention to right of stage when you're dancing. And I know this floor is small, and you have to compensate for that. But particularly when you hit each strong pose, presumably when you'll be in the spotlight, you've a tendency to prioritise the right rather than front of stage. If it was me, I'd focus more on the audience. Give them everything you've got, especially as it's one of your solo numbers.'

By now, Dair was nodding, agreeing with her. 'You're correct. When I'm dancing in the living room, I'm using all four walls equally, and it's the same in the dance studio. I need to think of a stage setting. Present to the audience more.'

They continued to work on this for the remainder of the afternoon.

Winding up the dance choreography as it was almost time to start getting ready for the radio show, Dair wanted to dance with Huntine.

'I'm dancing this routine with Shona,' he said. 'It's part waltz, part show dance. Would you like to try it?'

'Yes.' Huntine stepped on to the floor, expecting them to start in a traditional waltz hold.

'No, face the audience, then turn and look at me as I walk towards you.'

Huntine faced in the direction he'd suggested, and then, as the music kicked in, she turned around.

Dair walked towards her, taking long, elegant dancer's strides.

'Clasp your fingers in mine,' he instructed. 'Push me away, but I won't let you go. Then you let me wrap my arms around you, and take you in hold.'

Huntine felt herself react to the romance of the choreography, and then began to waltz with Dair around the floor until the music stopped. Again, her face was so close, gazing up at him, that he was tempted to take things further. To kiss her sweet lips.

'That was perfect,' he said, stepping back and bowing. 'Thank you for helping me with the choreography.'

'I hope I haven't meddled too much.'

'Not at all.' He checked the time. 'We'd better get ready. The studio isn't far, but the traffic could be busy.'

Packing up her laptop, she picked up her bag. Dair put on a clean white shirt, and then they headed outside.

They got into Dair's sleek, silver car and drove off.

The fading sunlight flickered through the trees in his garden as they headed away.

The traffic was busy, but they arrived on time at the studio, and were escorted to the guest room where Mullcairn gave them a warm welcome and was introduced to Dair.

'I read the press features and was hoping you'd come in for a chat,' Mullcairn said to them.

'We're delighted to be invited,' Huntine told the radio presenter.

'I've never been on the radio before,' Dair thought he'd clarify.

'Ah, you'll be fine,' Mullcairn assured him. 'You're a performer, and we've plenty to talk about. I'll begin with a wee introduction, then I'll use the highlights from the features to get the chatter going. I'm eager to talk to both of you about the new songs. Have you recorded any of your songs that I could play on the radio, Dair?'

'Not yet, but I'm in the process of doing this,' said Dair.

'Well, once you've got the songs recorded, send me a copy. I'll have a wee listen, and maybe have the two of you back on the show to chat some more. Probably before both of your tours, your shows, are up and running.'

'That would be wonderful,' said Dair.

Huntine smiled and nodded.

Someone signalled to Mullcairn that it was time to head into the studio to start the show.

They went through, and were set up with microphones and headphones, and the show's familiar introductory song began.

'We're having our usual phone–in,' Mullcairn told them. 'Are you up for taking a few calls from listeners?'

'Yes,' Huntine said. No hesitation.

Dair nodded and smiled, but felt the nerves kick in.

The music set the atmosphere for a cheery, lively show.

Dair glanced a few times at Huntine as they sat opposite Mullcairn. They could both feel the excitement building.

As the opening song finished, Mullcairn began...

'On the show this evening, I have a live interview with playwright and romance author, Huntine Grey. Apart from the launch of her latest play soon, the talented wordsmith has been up to something new and exciting — she's writing song lyrics for popular dancer, Dair. His new dance show goes on tour this summer, so not long now, and he's singing his own songs, playing piano and guitar. So we've got a lot of wonderful things to chat about on tonight's show.' Mullcairn sounded happy to be interviewing them. *'Stay tuned, we'll be chatting after this song...'*

The song started playing, allowing Mullcairn to chat to them off–air. 'Before we start. Will you be dancing with Dair at his shows?' he said to Huntine.

'No, I'm just helping him with his song lyrics,' she replied.

'Ach, I thought maybe you'd be performing. I remember you saying you had a background in all sorts of dancing,' said Mullcairn.

'Huntine is a lovely dancer,' Dair chimed–in. 'I only found out today that she can dance.'

Mullcairn looked surprised. 'You never knew Huntine could dance, even when she started writing your lyrics?'

'No.' Dair smiled. 'She kept that a secret.'

Mullcairn grinned. 'Oh, I want to hear all the gossip about this. And do you have a leading lady for your dance tour?' he added.

'Yes, I'm partnering with Shona,' Dair told him. 'I have three other couples dancing in the show too.'

The song finished and Mullcairn began...

'*For listeners wishing to phone–in with a question for Huntine, Dair, or for me, here is the number to call.*' Mullcairn announced the number. And then the interview began. '*Welcome, Huntine. It's lovely to have you back on the show.*'

'*Thank you, Mullcairn,*' she said.

'*I hear you've been extra busy with your writing,*' said Mullcairn. '*Your latest play is due to go on tour in theatres throughout Scotland this summer, and you'll be working again with Cambeul who directed your other plays. You're working on your next romance novel too. But I'm intrigued to find out that you're writing song lyrics for Dair. How did that come about?*'

Huntine summarised what had happened when they'd met at the dance studio.

'*What type of songs are they?*' Mullcairn wanted to know, bringing Dair into the conversation.

'*Popular music,*' said Dair. '*Romantic.*'

'*Oooh! Romance. I like the sound of that. Being a romantic at heart myself.*'

'*I wrote the music, and tried to write lyrics, but I'm not a writer,*' said Dair. '*Huntine has now written most of the lyrics. We were working on finishing some of the new songs today — and dancing.*'

'*Ah, yes, I hear you only found out today that Huntine can dance,*' said Mullcairn.

'*Yes, she kept it a secret, so as not to complicate our business agreement,*' Dair summarised.

Huntine glanced over at Dair, relieved he didn't reveal too much.

'*Although Huntine won't be dancing with me on stage at the shows, I think her understanding of dance has helped her write the lyrics that I was trying to express with my dancing. She's certainly added the romance that I was looking for.*' Dair then clarified. '*Romance for the songs.*'

Mullcairn cut–in. '*Remember, folks, phone in if you've a question for Huntine or Dair. And we'll be right back to chat more about dancing and romance after these wee jingles.*'

CHAPTER SEVEN

I changed my world around for you
I'd do it all again
Dance for the memories we shared
And could share again...

Huntine walked with Dair to his car after finishing the radio interview. The night air was calm, unlike them.

'That was a wild experience,' Dair said, framing it nicely. 'But I liked Mullcairn.'

Huntine nodded. 'I just didn't expect Cambeul to phone–in.' She wasn't sure if Cambeul had added anything other than nervous chatter.

'Or Shona,' Dair added, frowning. 'Did she have a question? Or did I miss it while she talked about how much she wanted to compete in the dance contests?'

'I didn't know she was eager to compete in the competitions with you,' said Huntine.

'Yes, but I don't want to step back into the competitive dance circuit,' he said firmly. 'Shona knows this.'

'Would the two of you have a chance of winning in this latest competition? Picking up a new title?'

He sighed heavily. 'Maybe. I think we could place in the contest. My nearest rival, he's a top–class dancer, with strong, stylish techniques. He's a favourite to win a few titles this year. His partner is a lovely dancer, but I'd rate Shona far better than her.'

'It sounds as if you and Shona could make a winning couple.'

Dair shook his head. 'I'm not stepping back into the contests. I want to push forward with the dance shows.'

They got into the car and Dair drove them back to his house.

When they arrived, Huntine dug her car keys out of her bag, ready to drive home.

'Would you like a cup of tea before you go?' he offered, opening the front door and inviting her in. 'Unwind, it's been a hectic day.'

Huntine took him up on his offer and followed him inside. She flopped down on the couch like a rag doll, and listened to him rattling around in the kitchen making the tea. The light from the kitchen shone through, adding to the cosiness of the table lamp's glow in the living room.

'Did you ever compete in the dance contests?' Dair called through to her while the kettle boiled and he set up the cups.

'No,' she called back. 'I didn't want to compete. I'm not the competitive type.'

She heard him guffaw and scoff.

'Not in that sense. I'm ambitious when it comes to my writing, but I never even wanted to perform on stage. I had the chance when I was a wee girl, and later on, but I didn't have that urge to be a performer in front of a live audience.' She wandered through to the kitchen. 'My gran loved the buzz of it, and I was there many a night at the sides of the stage, watching the actors and dancers in costume. But I prefer being in the background, the writer, happy to watch the actors and entertainers perform my plays.'

Dair stirred milk in their tea and handed a mug to her.

'Could we sit outside in the garden to drink our tea?' she requested, wanting to enjoy the calm atmosphere and the night air.

'Yes.' He led her outside to the garden. A patio table and two chairs were set up. They sat down, lit by the glow of a lantern and the light shining out from the kitchen window.

Huntine relaxed back and cupped her tea. 'This is lovely. I do envy you having a garden like this.'

'Pop round anytime while you're here in Edinburgh.'

'I might do that. You'd probably never know I was here. You never hear me knocking on the front door because you're always so busy with your kitchen cabaret.'

'I don't always dance and sing when I'm in the kitchen.'

Huntine eyed him in disbelief.

'Okay, so I do perform when I'm on my own and don't think anyone is watching me,' he confessed. 'But if you're going to be here more often, then I won't be inclined to dance on my own.'

Huntine nodded and took a sip of her tea.

As she put her mug down on the table, Dair clasped her hand and pulled her to her feet.

'No, Dair!' She giggled as he took her in hold and began to dance dramatically with her. Dipping her, he then wrapped her in his arms and waltzed her around the patio area outside the kitchen.

Her laughter filtered up into the clear night air, and she felt the drama of the radio show drift into the starry sky.

Breathless from laughter and being dipped and danced by Dair, Huntine sat down to finish her tea.

'What are you up to tomorrow? Any rehearsals at the studio?' he said.

'No rehearsals until the evening after that. So I'll be up early to tackle a full day's writing, working on my novel. What about you?'

'Dance rehearsals tomorrow night, so during the day, I'll practise the choreography. Though I expect to be overwhelmed with chatter from the other dancers about the features and radio interview.'

'I wish Cambeul hadn't brought up about your bare chest on Mullcairn's show.'

'Mullcairn made light of it.'

'Yes, but Cambeul has a bee in his bunnet about your tendency to take your shirt off.'

Dair checked the time. 'I haven't taken my shirt off for hours.' He pretended to undo more buttons on his shirt than the top two.

'Don't you dare, Dair!' she scolded him, and then they laughed.

He relaxed back, keeping his shirt buttoned.

'You enjoy teasing me, don't you? Well, fair warning,' she told him. 'One day I might take you up on your nonsense.'

'It's your fault. You bring out the rascal in me.'

She smiled over at him, and then drank the last of her tea. Gazing up at the glittering sky, she breathed in the scent of the flowers and greenery, and then stood up. 'Thanks for the tea, and the impromptu dance.'

He smiled and walked her to her car.

She was about to drive off when he leaned down and spoke to her through the open window. 'I know you're having a writing day tomorrow, but if you've time in the evening, come along to the dance rehearsal and see the choreography.'

Huntine smiled, without committing to a firm reply, and waved as she drove off.

Smirry rain cast the morning in a grey mist that made Huntine feel extra cosy sitting writing in her flat.

The outlines of Edinburgh's historic buildings were thrown into soft focus, taking the hard edges off and blended the past with the present.

She'd slept well and woke up early, and began writing before stopping to have breakfast. Porridge with creamy milk and a cup of tea.

Forging on with her novel, the words seemed to flow fast and fluent, and by the afternoon she'd written a chapter and was on to the next one. A productive writing day, even though her thoughts drifted to Dair and the fun they'd had the past few days, and nights.

She stopped to make afternoon tea and check her messages when she noticed that several emails had come through on her website. All from people she'd never met, involved in the world of publishing, theatre, dance and music, introducing themselves, having heard her on the radio and read about her work in the features. Offers were being presented to her, some lucrative, others ranging from intriguing to enticing, and a few wanting to meet her in person or have face–to–face chats on the phone.

So deep in thought about what she was reading, she jolted when Cambeul phoned her.

'I've had a few people message me regarding the play, and wondering what other plays are in the planning,' said Cambeul.

'So have I. I'm going to reply to them, asking for more information, or perhaps arranging a phone chat.'

They coordinated the contacts, realising that a few of those interested in the new plays were the same.

'The radio interview has certainly ignited a lot of interest in my writing,' said Huntine. 'As has the press features.'

'All to the good. Let me know if any of them follow through.'

'I'll do that,' she told him.

'You came across really well on the Mullcairn show.'

'Thank you, Cambeul. I didn't think you'd want to take part.'

'I didn't. I only phoned to leave a helpful question, but when they asked for my name and realised I was the director of your play, they put me right through to the live show. I could hear myself floundering. And I'm sure I sounded grumpy remarking on Dair being shirtless.'

'It's fine, and Dair's not fussed.'

'I'm glad. I don't want to ruffle feathers,' said Cambeul. 'And I don't know Shona, but she sounded miffed that Dair won't partner with her for the dance contest.'

'He's not interested in competing again.'

A call came through for Cambeul. 'I have to take this,' he said.

After chatting to Cambeul, Huntine replied to the messages, and then got on with her writing.

Later, she decided to take Dair up on his offer to pop along to the dance rehearsals. She'd worked on writing her book all day, and got ready to head to the studio.

Looking through her wardrobe, she put on a pair of classy ecru trousers and a beige blouse. Nothing that resembled leisure wear that could hint she wanted to join in with the dance rehearsals. She thought it would be inappropriate to turn up as if she expected to be part of the dance group now that her dancing skills were known.

Shrugging on her cream coat, she had her laptop with her and a notebook and pens in her bag to work on the lyrics. That's why she was invited to come along to the dancing, to see them perform, and hopefully get ideas to write the song lyrics.

She drove to her usual spot, parked the car, and then walked the short distance to the dance studio.

The energy of the city buzzed around her. She loved evenings like this, walking through the heart of Edinburgh under a vast velvety sky.

Lights from the cafes, bars, restaurants and other eateries shone bright and welcoming, and people were out enjoying themselves, making the most of the vibrant city.

A call came through on her phone and she smiled when she saw it was her grandfather, Jock.

'Huntine. I don't know if you've heard the news, but Dair's tour director has hired me on a freelance basis to help book more theatre venues for the dance shows,' he told her. 'I was happy to give him some contacts and tips, but then with all the publicity in the press and on the radio, ticket sales have soared, so they need to find a lot more venues now. And the tour director insisted on hiring me for the task.'

'That's wonderful! I'm on my way to Dair's dance rehearsals.'

'Jessy's delighted too. So I'm stepping out of my retirement for a wee bit during the summer, doing something I love. I wanted to thank you for suggesting me as an advisor.'

'I'm so pleased,' Huntine told him.

'Right, I'll let you get on with the rehearsals. We'll speak soon.'

Ahead, the entrance to the dance studio was lit up, and she walked up and went inside, following along the corridor that led to the dance room. Music sounded from inside, and she pushed the door open, hoping not to disturb the rehearsals.

Dair was partnered with Shona, and the other three couples were there too, performing a dramatic piece of choreography. They were all dressed in dancewear, and Huntine was glad she'd worn her stylish classics.

A few of them noticed her arrival, including Shona, but they continued to perform the routine.

Huntine sat down on a chair at the side of the room near the door, and watched the choreography. The song wasn't one of Dair's. It was a popular classic, one that audiences would enjoy.

Dair suddenly saw Huntine reflected in the mirror, and smiled at her, before picking Shona up for one of the lifts.

Huntine thought they danced well together, and that Shona was a skilful dancer. She'd checked the dance contest that Shona wanted to enter, and with a performance like this, they could probably walk away with the title. But this routine was obviously for the show. Though she could understand why Shona was eager to compete. The only thing she sensed was lacking, was an equal connection. Shona had real feelings of longing for Dair, while his were acted out as part of the routine. Only the trained eye would know this, or those familiar with their personal circumstances. On the surface, they were a perfect match, and the show would benefit from their partnership.

When the song finished, Dair came bounding over to Huntine while the dancers took a few minutes break.

'Did you hear the news about Jock?' Dair said, smiling as he approached. He wore a sky blue vest and dark dancewear trousers, and his muscles looked lithe and strong, from his broad shoulders down to his lean waist.

Huntine felt her heart flutter, and tried to push such feelings aside. 'Yes, my grandfather just phoned me.'

Dair placed his hands on his waist and took a deep breath from the exertion of the routine, particularly the lifts. 'I've been inundated with messages from people who'd listened to the radio show, and read the features. The publicity has created such a spark of interest. We need to book more theatres, and Jock's just the man we need. He's already sorted out two theatres on the west coast. Theatres we hadn't even considered.'

'My grandfather doesn't hang around. He's spent a lifetime working in the theatres and folk like him. He has plenty of contacts.'

'We're grateful to have him on board,' said Dair. Then he eyed her up and down. 'Did you bring your dance shoes with you?'

'I'm wearing a pair of ballroom shoes.'

He looked at her bag, hoping she'd brought a change of clothing. 'What about dancewear?'

Huntine put her hands out at her sides. 'I didn't come here to dance. It's not my place to do that.'

'Yes, but—'

Huntine cut–in. 'I came to see the choreography so that I can feel the drama, the story, and then write the lyrics. A few more verses and a chorus, and I think you'll have plenty of words to complete your songs.'

She saw his chest deflate, despite hiding his feelings behind a smile.

Realising that Huntine would be finished writing his lyrics soon, affected him stronger than he imagined. Would she still be in touch with him? Come over for lunch and dinner? His mind started to torment him, so he forced a brighter smile.

'Great,' he said. 'I should have the songs finished soon. Then I can record them in the music studio. My tour director has found a suitable studio that has a piano I can play, and he's made a provisional booking.' He stepped closer. 'I was hoping you'd find the time to come with me, after all, you wrote the lyrics to the songs that will be recorded.'

The look he gave her showed that he really wanted her to go with him. 'I'll go.'

'You're familiar with recording studios, so you can keep me right.'

Shona came over to join them.

Dair made the introductions.

Shona forced a smile as she eyed Huntine. She'd seen pictures of Huntine, and checked out her website. But seeing her here in the dance studio, and now realising that the writer was a dancer too, caused a ripple of potential rivalry.

Sensing Shona's reaction, Dair swept Huntine over to introduce her to the other dancers. They welcomed her warmly, and a couple of them commented that they'd listened to the radio interview and enjoyed the show.

'When Dair told us he'd invited you along tonight, I thought you'd be dancing with us,' Shona said to Huntine, sounding suspicious.

'No,' Huntine told her.

Shona's ponytail flicked, sensing an uneasy tension, but unsure how to handle it. Taking a bottle of water from her bag, she took a drink, and let the others continue the conversation.

'Okay, let's run through the number again,' Dair announced.

Huntine went back to the side of the room, sat down, and had her notebook ready to write any words that came to mind.

Dair turned the music on and ran over to take Shona in hold. A dramatic pose.

And then the energetic and dramatic performance began.

Shona's arm was draped around Dair's shoulders. The other dancers followed the same movements, all keeping in time to the lively song. Kicks and flicks, dancing across the floor, pivots and pirouettes.

When they finished, Dair walked over to Huntine. 'We're going to perform the opening number now. That's why I particularly wanted you to be here. To see how the show starts.'

Huntine listened as he continued to reveal the opening to the show.

'I'll stand at the side, while the dancers perform a ceilidh dance mix. The music is a basic recording of my opening song. I recorded it at home. For the show, I'll be singing and playing piano and guitar at the side of the stage while they appear out of the blue and purple lights and begin to dance.'

'I understand.'

'As the song finishes, another song, not one of mine, will play, and that's when I join the others for the big opening number.'

Huntine's heart beat excitedly in anticipation of seeing this.

Dair elaborated, spreading his arms out and gesturing to the things that would be included. 'We'll have atmospheric lighting, creating a Scottish mist effect, then the colours of the lights will increase as the mix of ceilidh dancing, Highland dancing and modern stage entwine in a rousing routine. Once I've finished singing, I'll join the others and perform part of a Scottish sword dance.'

Huntine's eyes lit up in anticipation. 'Will you be performing it tonight?'

'I will.' Dair gestured over to where two dance practise swords were ready for use. 'After a minute of sword dancing, the swords will be swept away, and we'll perform the group dance that opens the show.'

CHAPTER EIGHT

Dance on the wild side with me
Feel the strength of my love for you
Match each other's passion in the choreography
Feel it deep, feel it strong
Intertwine your moves with mine
Tango on the wild side with me...

Dair and the dancers performed a spectacular opening routine. Huntine had never seen choreography that combined ceilidh, Scottish Highland and stage dancing like this before. She recognised specific pieces of the popular ceilidh elements and Scottish dance moves. But Dair's own interpretation, combining traditional and modern dance, created contemporary choreography that set the room alight with energy and dazzling dance moves.

Huntine hardly dared to blink in case she missed a moment of it. And this was the effect it had on her without a stage setting, special lighting and costumes. She pictured Dair wearing his ghillie shirt and tight–fitting trews. Every strong, lithe muscle accentuated as he danced.

The other dancers were a close–knit team of talent and tenacity, skill and spectacle. Dair had selected the perfect team for his tour.

The number finished on a crescendo of ceilidh choreography, and although she hadn't danced a step, Huntine felt breathless from watching such an exciting performance.

She stood up and smiled as Dair strode towards her, sweeping his hair back from his forehead. 'What do you think of it?'

'Wow! Just wow!' Huntine enthused, causing the other dancers to smile over at her.

Shona sat down on the other side of the room and took a sip of water before tightening her ponytail and getting ready for the next number.

'Can you stay to watch the next routine?' Dair said to Huntine.

'Yes, though I don't know how much lyric writing I'll get done as I'm so distracted by the dancing,' she said.

Dair laughed and walked over to get ready for the next part of the rehearsal, partnering up with Shona for a ballroom waltz that merged into a modern stage routine.

Again, Huntine sat there and took in the excellent choreography and high level of dancing.

The dancers continued to rehearse for the next hour, before finally getting ready to leave.

Dair waved them off, and then he came over, pulled up a chair and sat down close to Huntine, barely out of breath.

She held up her blank notebook.

'So you enjoyed the show then,' he said, smiling at her.

'From start to finish.'

'And that's just part of the show,' he reminded her.

'I think you've done an incredible job with the choreography. I love the interweaving of traditional and modern dance. And your popular song choices. You made me want to get up and dance.'

'Come on then.' Dair stood up and clasped her hand. 'Dance with me.'

Huntine leaned back. 'You must be exhausted.'

He gazed down at her, his eyes shining like pale sapphires. 'Do I look tired?'

'No, but—'

'One dance, and then we'll go home.'

She wondered if he'd noticed what he'd inferred, but didn't pick him up on it. They would be going home. To separate accommodation.

His gentle strength manoeuvred her to the centre of the floor, facing the wall of mirrors. He leaned close to her ear and whispered. 'Since you're wearing your dance shoes...'

His words, his breath, sent sensual shivers down her neck.

'All my shoes are dance shoes. I didn't wear them tonight for dancing.'

He smiled and stepped away to put on some music. 'Did you study the routines?'

'I took them in, but I—'

'What one would you like to dance with me?' he cut-in.

Huntine shrugged, letting him choose. She had taken in the routines, but only at a watch–once level. Though years of dance training had given her an edge when it came to picking up choreography.

The song started to play, and she could hear from the introduction that they were about to tackle the tango routine that combined traditional steps with Dair's own flamboyant flair.

Wearing the blue vest that emphasised his broad shoulders and lean torso, Dair walked over to her and took her in hold.

'I'm not wearing a red dress,' she reminded him as they got ready to tango.

'One night you will.' His firm lips spoke with such assurance that a rush of feelings swept over her.

Her fingers felt the muscles in his bare arms and shoulders, igniting further flutterings. She wondered if she should forgo the tango. It was surely inviting intimacy she wasn't ready for.

But as the seconds ticked down, Huntine pushed all her practical objections aside and decided tonight she'd let herself dance on the wild side.

Dair took charge of the opening of the dance, and Huntine followed his lead. She'd always loved the tango, and the strength of her passion for the dance showed through as they began to match each other's movements.

Dancing the tango with Huntine secretly took Dair aback. He'd imagined they'd dance it well. But having danced it earlier with Shona, and thinking he'd felt the passion in the choreography, Huntine just raised the bar. Or perhaps it was the added attraction he felt deeply for the wordsmith. Passion that didn't exist in his heart for Shona.

Huntine's kicks and flicks, as they intertwined their limbs, felt like two lovers enticing each other. And the way those gorgeous grey eyes of hers looked up at him, affected him in ways he hadn't felt in a long time.

The urge to kiss her, as part of the dance, to claim her as his own, were almost too much to resist. Somehow, he kept his temptations in check, until the last few movements of the dance.

It wasn't deliberate, but as she turned her head away from him, dancing the choreography, as if they'd had a lovers' tiff, and he'd cupped her face to gaze at him, his lips brushed against hers.

A searing moment. Unintentional, but unforgettable.

The spark between them was unmissable.

Huntine reacted. Had he kissed her? He had, if a brush of the lips could be construed as such. She could tell from the look in his eyes he wondered if she'd rebuke him or respond in kind.

She did neither, pretending she'd barely noticed, and danced on until the final notes of the song hung in the air, and he dipped her full and strong.

Leaning back, trusting his strong arms to hold her tight, she leaned all the way, arching her back in a balletic stretch, one arm draped out, fingers pointing away.

They lingered for a second in this dramatic pose, and then he lifted her up, righting her. Dair then bowed slowly and stepped back.

'Thank you for dancing with me, Huntine.' His voice sounded ragged from the feelings she'd stirred in him.

She smiled, her heart thundering, still feeling the touch of his lips brushing against hers.

And then song lyrics began to flicker through her thoughts. She hurried over, grabbed her notebook and pen, and started to write the words down before they faded like her night with Dare was due to do.

Dair started to pack up his bag, and shrugged a top on over his vest.

'It's only three lines,' Huntine said, handing him the notepad.

He smiled and nodded as he read them. 'Ideal for the missing piece of the verse we were working on.'

'We should be almost done with the lyrics.'

'Yes, I'll try to play through the three songs and see what's left to write. Your lyrics have been so much better than mine that I find myself replacing them with yours. I need to sit down at my piano and sort through the final selection of lyrics.'

'I'll tidy these up and send you a polished copy.' She tucked the notepad in her bag and they both got ready to leave.

As he went to turn the lights off, he saw Huntine reflected in the mirrors. Unaware that he was looking at her, she put her coat on.

He felt a pang of longing, feeling the emptiness already when she had to go back to her own life and he got on with his, without her.

Dair turned off the lights and followed Huntine out of the dance room, along the corridor and out into the night. A few people were meandering along, while the buzz of the city murmured in the background. And the lights shone in the distance from Edinburgh castle.

As he walked with her back to her car that was parked near his, he repeated the new lyrics she'd written.

'I like the feeling of romance and longing in your lyrics,' he said. And then he began to sing the words.

Everyone was too wrapped up in their own business to mind about Dair serenading Huntine.

Huntine listened to his rich, musical voice sound clear in the evening air.

'The lyrics work well with this verse,' he said, and then proceeded to give her an encore.

'I'll add them to the remainder of the song's lyrics and send you a finished copy,' she said.

By now, they'd reached her car and she got in while he spoke to her through the window.

'By the way, I've finished reading your book. I thoroughly enjoyed it. I really like your writing.'

'Thank you, Dair.'

'The features should be published in the paper's magazine supplement tomorrow,' he reminded her.

She hadn't forgotten. 'We should gear up for more messages and offers to pop up from this next round of publicity.'

'Are there any new offers you've taken up?' he said.

'I've replied to a few, but there are a couple that I'd like to discuss further. A theatre in Edinburgh is interested in reading any romantic Christmas plays I have, or could create in time for a festive show.'

'I hope that works out. You'd have to stay in Edinburgh a lot longer. Maybe even move to the east coast.'

'We'll still be in touch, probably, when I go home to Glasgow. And it's not that far to drive.'

'No probably about it.'

His smile warmed her heart.

'Do you have a Christmas play written?' he said.

'I have. I finished it months ago, but the current plays took centre stage with my work. I'll have a read through my writing archives and refresh myself with the storyline of the play, the characters, and I vaguely remember adding in ballroom dancing.'

'There's dancing in your Christmas romance play!' He sounded interested.

'One routine for a romantic scene. I might add more dancing to the script. You've sparked my dancing past.' She thought about the other offers she'd had for her writing. 'I always have several projects on the boil as it keeps my writing fresh and exciting. And another theatre wants to chat to me about my new plays.' She put the focus on him. 'What about you? Any offers that entice you?'

He nodded. 'Theatres want me to do another run of the dance show tour later in the year, around Christmastime. I'm discussing this with my tour director.'

'It sounds like we're both going to be extra busy. Happily so,' she said.

'Okay, I'll let you go and get on with writing your novel, and a romantic Christmas play.'

'And the song lyrics,' she reminded him.

Dair burst into song, serenading her as she drove off waving to him.

The temperature of the night didn't alter, but Dair felt a cold draft blow by his heart. One day Huntine would be driving off for the foreseeable future, and he knew his heart was in jeopardy of missing her.

Pushing away thoughts that felt heavy on his shoulders, he hummed the song and muttered the lyrics as he walked to his car.

Driving through the city to the outskirts, he sang in the confines of the car, raising his voice to a crescendo. By the time he'd parked outside his house, he felt he'd finished the song.

Heading into the living room, he flicked a lamp on and sat down at his piano. In the glow of the light, he played the tune and sang the final words of the lyrics that completed the song.

Then he recorded himself and played it again.

Later, a polished copy of the lyrics came through on a message from Huntine.

He read them and replied. *Thank you. They complete the song perfectly.*

In her flat, Huntine sat at the window with her laptop, writing. Edinburgh glistened with lights, and the glow from the city reflected upwards into the starry sky.

Another message came through from Dair. *Writing late?*

Huntine took a picture of her view from the window and sent it to him with her message. *A view from my writing garret. Such a beautiful night.*

Dair looked at the picture. He'd wondered what her flat was like, her wee world, tucked away from the hustle and bustle where she could write. *Truly beautiful*. And so was Huntine, he thought to himself. *I had a great night dancing the tango with you.*

So did I. I'll keep a lookout for a red dress from the vintage clothes shop. They sell pretty pre–loved fashion. Maybe even a hot pink one too.

Buy both. Let's dance as often as we can before our tours start this summer.

I will. Goodnight, Dair.

Goodnight, Huntine.

Dair sat playing his piano, unwinding before getting ready for bed. But he couldn't get the feeling of dancing with Huntine out of his thoughts. Opening the patio doors, he let the fragrant night air waft in, and played the melodies he'd perform on stage fairly soon.

The routines, the choreography, the songs...everything was all coming together as he'd hoped and planned. Though he hadn't planned on meeting the mesmerising Huntine Grey.

CHAPTER NINE

I'm glad I risked a broken heart
One hot summertime
Although it seems so long ago
I never really let you go
In my heart I'm still yours
And you are mine...

The city of spires shone in the morning sunlight against the blue sky as Huntine walked to the grocery shop to check if the features were in the magazine.

The shop was fairly busy with customers. Huntine went in and noticed that the newspaper's magazine supplement was propped up on the stand for sale with the paper.

Her heart skipped a beat when she saw that the picture of her smiling with Dair while he played the piano had made it to the front cover. Four thumbnail pictures advertised the magazine's contents, and they were highlighted at the top of the cover and were captioned — *Dairing Dancing Duo Tune–up*.

Huntine picked up two copies of the paper with the magazines. One for herself. And one to keep on hand in case her parents, who were away from the Highlands on business, wanted a copy.

She grabbed a plain sliced loaf, milk and tattie scones and took her items up to the counter.

The grocer smiled as he put her items through the till. 'Are you in the newspaper?'

Huntine blinked. How did he know?

'Folk usually only buy two copies of the paper when they're in it,' he explained without her asking.

She smiled tightly. 'Yes.'

The grocer looked at the front cover of the paper. She hadn't noticed that it advertised the magazine supplement. So they'd technically made the front page of the paper too. He glanced from the picture to Huntine, comparing the faces.

'Oh! You're the dancing lassie,' he assessed, so loudly that several customers instantly took an interest in her.

Rather than clarify that she was the writer and Dair was the dancer, Huntine nodded, smiled and paid for her groceries, hoping to make a speedy exit. She wasn't averse to the publicity, but she wasn't up for scrutiny from well–meaning strangers.

Being a writer, even a fairly successful one, was like wearing a cloak of invisibility. Nobody really recognised her as the writer of the plays, but were au fait with the leading actors and even Cambeul the director. And she was fine with that. She didn't seek the spotlight, but this morning she was standing in the full glare, trying to make a run for it with her magazines and tattie scones.

'Do you know Dair?' one of the ladies in the queue said to her.

Before she could reply, the grocer was thumbing through the magazine at speed and stabbed a delighted finger when he came to the features. 'There you are with Dair. He's playing the piano while you're singing.'

'I'm not singing, I'm smiling—' Huntine tried to clarify, but the customers bustled around her, wanting to see the features.

'Is Dair the dancer dating a singer now?' another woman asked her friend, eager for gossip.

Huntine hadn't quite realised the strength of Dair's notoriety, and found herself in the eye of their interest for snippets of gossip about the handsome dancer.

'When does his dance tour start?' yet another woman said.

This was one question that Huntine could answer. 'The beginning of next month, through the summertime. Touring all over Scotland. The dates, times and ticket availability are on Dair's website.'

Two women gasped. 'It's nearly the end of the month. We'd better get our tickets bought.'

In the melee, Huntine made a smiling but hasty exit. Speed walking away from the grocery shop, she slowed down outside the window of the vintage clothes shop. The owner was wrestling one of the mannequins to put a hot pink dress on it.

Huntine hurried inside to save her the trouble.

'Can I try the pink dress on? If it's my size.'

The owner looked relieved and showed how much stretch there was in the body–hugging fabric. 'It's a retro dress. A designer eighties number. Bright and bold. Small to medium size with plenty of stretch. You've a neat figure. It would fit you.'

Huntine tried it on in the changing room. The bubblegum pink was so hot it threw a rosy glow on to everything it reflected in the mirror. Her first inclination was to take it off and rummage the rails for something less vibrant. Flicking her hair back and straightening her shoulders, she reassessed her snap decision.

'Would you be interested in this too?' The woman assistant handed in a shimmering silver cocktail dress.

Huntine clasped the hanger and held the dress up. Silver was more her style. She upped her grey scale to sparkling silver for special occasions, especially Christmas parties.

'Yes, thanks, I'll try it on too.' Slipping out of the hot pink into the silver, she recognised herself. 'I'll take the silver. And the pink,' she forced herself to add before she changed her mind. 'Do you have any red dresses? Something suitable for a tango.'

'Oh, yes. It came in yesterday and it's a stoater.' The assistant hurried away and Huntine heard the hangers being flicked through, and then a hand reached in and dangled the most gorgeous, sexy, and bright scarlet dress Huntine could've hoped for into the changing room.

Chiffon, satin and soft stretch velvet combined to create a figure–flattering classy dress. The hemline tapered below mid–calf, with a slight split. The front of the bodice had a sweetheart neckline and shoestring straps. The back dipped low on the waist with scarlet sparkle sprinkled all the way down to the hips. The stretch in the fabrics ensured it skimmed the figure.

'Thanks, I'll try it on.' Huntine sounded calm, but her heart was racing. She slipped the silver dress off and put the red dress on. 'Wow!' One word was all it took for her to decide.

'All the dresses have been cleaned,' the assistant added. 'And I'd say from the few repairs we made before selling them, mainly to tidy the hems or missing sequins, they've only been worn once or twice.'

'I'll take all three dresses,' Huntine called through, putting her grey trousers and white blouse back on.

'Buying yourself a whole new wardrobe for the summer?' the assistant said cheerily, carefully folding the three dresses and putting them in a bag.

'Yes, stepping out of my usual neutrals.'

The assistant tallied up the cost and Huntine blinked at the bargain buys.

'That's the beauty of buying vintage dresses like these. They're real bargains. The quality is excellent, and the designs and fabrics are lovely.'

Huntine paid and picked up the bag. 'Thank you for your help.'

The assistant smiled and then frowned. 'Do I know you from somewhere?'

'I bought the turquoise dress in the window.'

'I remember that, but I feel like I've seen you somewhere.'

Huntine saw the newspaper and magazine behind the counter. 'I've been in the news with Dair, the dancer, he's—'

'Gorgeous. So handsome. My daughter and I have tickets for his new show. We saw him dancing in another tour last year. What a mover he is!'

'Yes, well, I hope you enjoy the show.'

'Tell him he'd make our night if he gave us a wave.' The woman named the date and theatre tickets she'd booked.

'I'll tell him.'

'Thanks so much. I know he might not, but it's worth an asking.'

'It is.' Huntine smiled and then left the shop, blinking against the sunlight and from the whirlwind of just popping out for the magazine.

When she got back to her flat, she hung the dresses up in her wardrobe, and sent a message to Dair telling him the magazine was out.

She'd started to make porridge for breakfast when Dair called her.

'I've got a copy of the magazine. I'm adding it as a news update to my website,' he said.

Huntine told him about the reaction to the features in the shops, including that she'd bought three dresses, and that the vintage clothes shop assistant requested a shout out during the show.

'You have been busy,' he said. 'And I'll make a note to give the shop assistant a mention,' he added.

'So now I'm going to get on with my writing,' she said. 'I have rehearsals for the play this evening.'

'I'm working on finishing the songs. I need them ready for the recording studio. No dance rehearsals tonight. But now I'll have to think up what dances we'll attempt when you wear the pink dress and the silver one. I'm thinking a quickstep for the silver, and a cha–cha–cha for the pink. Or a silvery salsa and a hot pink pasodoble.'

Huntine laughed.

The call ended on a cheery note, and Huntine made tea to go with her porridge, and then began working on her book.

During the next week, Huntine and Dair's paths rarely crossed at the dance studio. But the days whizzed by, until it was time for Dair to pack his guitars in his car, pick Huntine up and drive them to the music studio to record the new songs.

He carried both guitars as they headed into the studio where the sound proofing of the recording room cut the noise from the outside world.

'I'm starting to feel nervous,' Dair whispered to Huntine as the sound engineer set everything up. The hire included the use of a piano, a producer to advise on the recording, and mixing and mastering services. All arranged by Dair's tour director.

'That's okay,' she whispered. 'You'll settle once you start to play the piano and guitars. Try the piano, get a feel for it while the engineer sets things up,' she advised.

'Do you have your music and lyric sheets with you?' the producer said to Dair.

'Yes.' Dair held them up.

'Take a seat at the piano, set up your sheet music. We'll have a run through of your first song to test the sound and quality. Then we'll dive right into the recording of song one.'

Huntine smiled reassuringly at Dair, and then went through to a separate room, the control room, where she could watch him through the studio window.

Dair sat down at the piano, put his sheets on the stand, and played the piano, getting a feel for it. The style was similar to his own, and he felt comfortable playing the first song.

'We'll record you singing and playing the piano,' the producer told Dair, speaking to him via the control room. 'Then we'll record you playing guitar. Electric I think it is for this number.'

'Yes,' Dair confirmed.

Huntine sensed a change in Dair's manner, as if the professional performer in him rose to the fore when he needed to sing and play to the high standard needed for the recording.

She remained calm, and didn't do anything that would distract him.

It was one of the best renditions of the song she'd heard from him.

When Dair finished, the producer spoke through to him. 'I think we got that in one. But do you want to run through it again?' he offered.

'No, I'm happy with that,' said Dair. 'It felt right. I'll play my guitar now.'

The process was repeated with Dair playing electric guitar.

Huntine loved the tone and resonance of the guitar and again it seemed as if Dair had nailed it in one.

'Give me a couple of minutes to play this back,' the producer said to Dair.

While the producer replayed the music, to check the recording, Dair glanced through at Huntine. She smiled and gave him a nod.

Dair could see her genuine reaction, and the remnants of his nerves faded, to be replaced by eagerness to give the songs everything he had.

There was a short break midway through the recording session for tea and a chat, and then the work began again. The first two songs were in the bag, and the third was almost finished. Dair just had to play acoustic guitar as well as electric on this track. The piano was included on all three tracks.

Dair was still buzzing as he headed out of the studio carrying his guitars and walked to his car with Huntine. The night air was mild and refreshing.

Despite nailing the songs and playing on the initial rounds, the studio time that had been scheduled was all used up. Nothing was cut short. Everything was done to Dair's satisfaction, and he eventually left with the audio files, professionally recorded versions of his songs that would be made available for purchase and download from Dair's website.

He put his guitars in the boot of the car and then drove them away from the music recording studio.

The lights of the city flickered through the windows, and they both started to relax. Huntine hadn't realised how tense she'd been until she started to unwind.

'Thanks for coming with me as back–up,' he said. 'Now all we need is to video the full dress rehearsal run through of the dance show.'

'I'm really looking forward to seeing that,' she said. Dair had invited her, and Cambeul, to be in the handful of audience members when the show was performed in the stage room.

'All the costumes are finished. The final fittings were a couple of days ago,' he said.

'Are you still wearing your ghillie shirt and trews for the opening number?'

'I am. The costume designer has found me a pair of vintage trews, dark tartan trousers.'

'A ghillie shirt and tartan trews! You'll open the show in style wearing those.'

Dair threw her a sexy smile, and then continued to drive them through the vibrant heart of Edinburgh.

CHAPTER TEN

Dare to dance with me
Under a starlit night
Wrap yourself around me
Until the starlight turns to sunlight...

'Do you want to have supper with me?' Dair offered as they drove through the leafy outskirts of Edinburgh, leaving the buzz of the city's nightlife behind them.

Huntine glanced over at him.

'Nothing fancy,' he added, before she could refuse for all sorts of practical reasons. It was late, they'd had a long day and night, concluding with the recording session at the music studio. They both had early starts the next morning.

She frowned, pretending to be unimpressed. 'Cheesy toast?'

His lips curved into a smile, knowing she was teasing him. 'If that's what you want. But I could add my speciality to tonight's menu.'

'What's your speciality?'

He hesitated. 'Ah, well, it's sort of a surprise supper.' He'd have to check what was in the cupboards and the fridge. Hopefully, he hadn't wolfed down what he needed.

'A pot luck supper,' she surmised playfully.

'Exactly,' he said, playing along.

'Okay.' She leaned back in her seat.

Dair smiled and drove on to his house.

When they arrived, Dair insisted Huntine relax in the living room while he rustled up supper.

She wandered through to the living room and opened the patio doors and breathed in the evening air.

He checked the fridge and was relieved to find that he hadn't eaten all the fresh eggs he'd bought and began to make the omelettes. He beat the eggs in a bowl, melted a knob of butter in a pan, and poured the egg mix in to cook.

'These past few days, there's been a hint of summer in the air,' she called through to him.

He called back to her while adding grated cheese, salt and black pepper to the first omelette. 'I've been so busy, I've barely had time to relax and appreciate the spring. Now, we're getting nearer to the summertime, and the start of the tour.'

'Not long now.'

'Or for the start of your play.' Serving the omelette on to a warm plate, he started to make the second one while the kettle boiled for the tea.

'At least you've got your songs recorded.'

'Yes.' He sounded relieved. 'I'll give you a copy.'

'Thanks.' She heard a lot of frantic rustling and rattling going on in the kitchen. 'Want a hand?'

'Nope.' He garnished the omelettes with a sprinkling of parsley and set the plates on the kitchen table while he made the tea. Pouring two mugs of tea, he called through to her. 'Supper is ready.'

Huntine walked through to find him buttering two thick–cut slices of fresh crusty bread.

She'd guessed from the sounds coming from the kitchen, and the tasty aroma wafting through, that he was making omelettes. But she hadn't expected them to look so delicious.

'I'm impressed,' she said, sitting down at the table.

Dair lifted his mug of tea and smiled. 'Cheers!'

'Cheers!' She tipped her mug against his, and then they tucked into their tasty supper.

'My tour director has organised a photo–shoot here tomorrow morning,' he revealed. 'Publicity shots for the release of the songs on the website, which he's helping with too. We want to get them up as soon as possible. The pictures are to help promote the songs, and one will be used as the music cover.'

'I assume you'll be pictured playing the piano for the cover shot.'

'Yes, and the photographer will take pictures of me playing the guitars. It'll all be done in one photo–shoot.'

'I won't stay too long so you can get some sleep.'

Dair shook his head. 'I'm still buzzing from the day, the recording studio, everything, so I'm glad of your company to chat and unwind. Unless you need to dash.'

'I'm in no hurry.'

He smiled over at her. One of those unintentional sexy smiles that set her heart fluttering.

She lifted up a slice of bread and butter and took a bite.

Dair continued to chat. 'I was wondering, as you wrote the lyrics for the songs, and you'll be named as the lyricist in the credits, would you like to pop over in the morning and have a couple of photos taken with me? It's okay if you don't, but we'd like to include you in the publicity pictures.'

She found herself nodding. And wondering what she should wear. 'What are you wearing for the photos?'

'My ghillie shirt and trews. The outfit I'll be wearing for the opening dance routine after I've played the first song.'

'I'll wear my neutrals, to tone in. Or maybe my turquoise dress.'

'Yes, it's lovely, so certainly wear it.'

They finished eating their supper, and then went through to drink their tea in the living room.

Dair flicked another lamp on, and that's when she noticed that his trews were draped over a chair near the piano. They were made from a dark tartan. Black Isle tartan.

'I was breaking in my trews,' said Dair.

Huntine smiled. 'I've heard of people breaking in their shoes, but never breaking in their trews.'

'Earlier today I was rehearsing the dances. I wore the trews to see if they have enough stretch in them for the opening number. They felt great, and the ghillie shirt is ideal too. We'll be starting dress rehearsals in the dance studio soon. Any alterations needed will be made to the costumes.'

'All the costumes are ready for the play. Cambeul has scheduled a full dress rehearsal soon at the studio.'

She finished her tea, and wandered over to the open patio doors.

Dair stood beside Huntine as she gazed out at the garden and breathed in the scent of the greenery in the evening air.

He breathed it in too. 'It does feel like summer. And a busy one for both of us. New tour dates have been added again. Jock's helped us secure other theatre bookings.'

Huntine looked up at the stars twinkling in the night sky. 'Your songs being released are going to attract even more attention to your show. Remember to send me a copy of them.'

'I will.'

She sighed wearily. 'I'd better head home.'

Dair picked up his car keys and they went out to his car.

He drove her home, and during the short drive they chatted about the photo–shoot.

'I'll see you in the morning,' she said as he pulled up outside her flat.

'Come over for breakfast, if you want,' he offered. 'Nothing fancy. We've eaten all the tasty stuff.'

'I'll bring something tasty,' she said, planning to pick up items from the grocery shop.

She got out of the car, and Dair waited until she was inside, giving her a wave before driving off.

When he arrived home, he got ready for bed, and put on a pair of silk pyjama bottoms.

Lying in bed, his mind whirred with thoughts of everything that had happened during the busy day. And Huntine. He couldn't settle for thinking about her. If he wasn't careful, he could so easily fall in love with her.

Throwing the duvet back, he got out of bed, put a pair of dance shoes on, and went through to the living room.

By the glow of a lamp, he danced around the floor, burning off his excess energy, moving to the lively music, merging his show's choreography with impromptu kicks and spins, leaping across the floor.

Finally, he went back to bed, and fell into a deep sleep, and didn't wake until the first light of the bright early morning.

Huntine arrived carrying a bag of groceries. She knocked on the kitchen door, seeing Dair putting the kettle on to boil for tea.

He welcomed her in. 'You look lovely in your turquoise dress.'

She smiled. He hadn't yet put on his ghillie shirt and trews, and was wearing a white vest and training trousers, and she rightly assumed he'd been practising his dancing. But he was clean–shaven and his hair was swept back from his forehead as if he'd just stepped out of the shower and casually finger dried it.

She started to unpack the groceries. 'I've brought a selection of scones — a fruit, soda and treacle scone.'

'A treacle scone! I haven't had one of those in ages,' he said, peering at the items as she unpacked them.

'Eggs to replace the ones we scoffed.' She handed him a box of fresh eggs and he put them in the fridge. 'And butter, milk, yoghurt and cream.'

He added those too. 'I must make supper for you more often. I'd never need to go grocery shopping again.'

Huntine smiled and lifted two punnets of fruit from the bag. 'Raspberries and strawberries.' She glanced at his fruit bowl on the dresser. 'I noticed you had plenty of bananas and apples.'

'I'll start preparing a breakfast feast,' he said, peaking into the bag. 'What else did you buy?'

'A plain loaf and slices of Lorne sausage.'

'I'll fire up the grill.'

Huntine buttered slices of bread ready for the grilled, square slices of sausage, and started to make the tea.

Dair added slices of tomato to the grill and everything was cooking nicely.

She poured two mugs of tea and they sat down at the kitchen table to tuck in.

He checked the time. 'We're on schedule.'

They ate their breakfast, and apart from being distracted by the muscled shoulders and arms on view opposite her, she found herself feeling more relaxed in Dair's company than was probably good for her. Becoming accustomed to being with him here in his house wasn't the wisest move if she wanted to keep romance on the back burner this summer. Not that she thought Dair would want to date her. A summer fling wasn't part of their busy schedule.

'Penny for them.' He looked over the rim of his tea at her.

She jolted, and a blush threatened to form on her cheeks. 'Just thinking about the photo–shoot,' she lied.

His eyes remained on her, and she sensed he knew she was lying.

'I'm starting to read you better these days, and I think you're telling fibs.'

Her blush couldn't be contained any longer.

'You're blushing.'

'It's the heat in the kitchen.' And the heat of his gaze, knowing she wasn't being truthful. 'Does the photographer know I'm joining you?' she said, changing the conversation back to business.

'Yes, he knows you're taking part. And my tour director has arranged for him to take a few video clips of my singing and playing the piano and guitar while he's here. It would be great if you were up for being included in a clip. They're for the website.'

'What would you want me to do?'

'Stand near the piano, hold the sheet music, look like you're part of the whole process of the songwriting,' he said. 'The photographer will probably have suggestions.'

'I'll do it,' she agreed.

They were chatting about the theatre play, the dance tour, and the costumes when a message came through on Dair's phone.

He blinked in mild panic when he read it. 'The photographer is on his way. He'll be here in five minutes.'

Huntine jolted. 'He's early!'

Dair checked the time. 'No, we've been so busy nattering that he's on time. We're running late.'

Jumping up, Huntine started to clear the dishes over to the sink.

'Leave them. Help me get things ready.'

'What can I do?' Huntine was eager to help.

'Open the patio doors in the living room.'

Huntine ran through and pushed the doors open wide, letting in the fresh, morning air.

As she turned around quickly to check that the living room was tidy, Dair came dashing in, dressed only in a pair of boxer shorts and socks.

They bumped into each other, and she gasped as her hands pressed against the wall of lean muscle on his bare chest.

'Oh!' she said, stepping back.

Dair grabbed the tartan trews from the back of the chair where he'd left them the previous night, and dashed away to get dressed in his bedroom.

Huntine ran her hands through her hair, clearing her embarrassing thoughts.

Picking up bits and pieces, she shoved them in the drawers of a dresser, and then turned around and bumped into the dashing dancer again. He wore the trews, but still hadn't put his shirt on.

'Have you seen my ghillie shirt? I can't find it in my bedroom. I must've left it in here.'

They both scanned the living room and found no trace of the shirt.

'It has to be in your bedroom. I'll help you look,' she said, hearing the mild panic in her voice as the minutes ticked down before the photographer arrived.

He ran upstairs to his bedroom, winning by a narrow margin as she kept up with him. She joined in with his frantic search for the ghillie shirt through his wardrobe and chests of drawers.

'I've found it!' Huntine exclaimed, holding it up on a hanger. 'It was under one of your jackets.'

Dair let go the tense breath he'd been holding in. 'Great!' Unhooking it, he proceeded to pull it over his head, getting himself into a tussle in his rush to put it on. 'The laces are in a fankle,' he muttered.

Huntine unravelled the mess of the laces, and then left him to put it on and lace the front up, or enough not to show too much bare chest.

She couldn't help noticing that his bed was neatly made, and despite the current melee, his house was kept tidy.

The bedroom window was open and they heard a car pull up outside.

'That'll be him,' he gasped. He hadn't laced the shirt up yet or ran a brush through his hair. Or put his brogues on.

'I'll welcome him in,' Huntine offered, much to Dair's relief, and ran back downstairs.

Smoothing her hands down her dress, she shook her hair back, and tried not to look like she'd been wrestling a bare–chested hunk as she opened the front door.

'Dair's taking a call in his room,' she lied, leading him inside and through to the living room. 'He'll be down in a minute.'

The photographer was a man in his thirties, wearing a casual suit and had a friendly manner. He eased the heavy bag filled with photographic equipment off his shoulder and sat it down in the living room.

130

'That's fine. I'll do a quick light check.' He took a gadget from his pocket and started to click it around the room, gauging the light balance for the photos.

'Would you like a cup of tea?' Huntine offered.

'That would be great. I've been up since the crack of dawn. There was a beautiful pink and amber sky arching over Edinburgh castle at first light, and I was up to take pictures of it. Breakfast was a slurp of tea.'

Huntine smiled and headed through to the kitchen to make him a cup of tea, thinking he'd continue setting up for the photo–shoot. But he'd tagged along with her, and when she turned around after filling the kettle, he was standing there in the kitchen eyeing up the scones.

'Is that a treacle scone?' he said as she set up a mug for him.

'It is. Would you like a scone with your tea?' She couldn't very well not offer as he looked hungrily at them. 'There's a nice fruit scone and a large soda scone.'

'Treacle would be great, thanks. Just a wee slather of butter for me. I like to taste the treacle.'

Smiling tightly, Huntine buttered the treacle scone and put it on a plate. 'What do you take in your tea?'

'Milk, one sugar.'

The photographer was standing in the kitchen holding a mug of tea in one hand, and the buttered scone in the other when Dair walked in, surprised to find them there.

'I haven't had a treacle scone in ages,' the photographer said, taking a bite out of it and nodding that it was tasty.

Dair glared at him and then at Huntine, but forced himself to hide his ire that he'd been beaten to the treacle scone by the photographer.

'Do you want another cup of tea to wet your whistle for your singing?' Huntine said to Dair.

'Yes, thanks,' he said.

Huntine poured him a cup and handed it to him while the photographer made short work of the scone.

'Shall we go through to the living room?' said Dair, leading the way.

'That's a beautiful baby grand piano,' the photographer remarked. 'Your tour director told me he wants it highlighted in the pics. And your electric guitar.' The man glanced around and then saw the guitars on a stand near the piano.

'Yes, it's particularly for the front cover of my new songs that I've recorded,' said Dair.

'I'm going to one of your dance shows in Edinburgh,' the photographer told Dair. 'And I've booked tickets for your play that's showing in one of the city's theatres,' he said to Huntine. 'I read your features in the press and I love a night out at the theatre. And I like a drama with intrigue. Are you working on any new plays?'

'I am. I've another play in the works with Cambeul, the director. And I'm currently in discussions with another theatre about a Christmas play,' she said while the photographer set up his lights.

'I'll look out for those, Huntine.' He turned to Dair. 'Right, could you sit at your piano so I can get a few shots of you on your own. Then I'll ask Huntine to come into the frame.'

Huntine lifted the music sheets Dair had left for her on the coffee table, and clasped them ready to join in the photo–shoot.

'I'll take the photos first, and then film the video clips,' the photographer told them. 'This is a nice room. Plenty of light, stylish, and with the piano and guitars for your music and the dance floor. Do you mind if I ask — are you a couple? It'll let me create the right story with the pics.'

Huntine's eyes widened and she glanced at Dair. He was taken aback, and she was the first to reply. 'No.'

The photographer seemed surprised. 'I just thought that you both seemed so at home here. I hope you don't mind me saying. I want to create the right atmosphere for the photos.'

'We're just working together,' Huntine added. She heard herself sound unconvincing.

Dair smiled and nodded.

The photographer didn't press them further, and although he didn't know Huntine, he sensed she was spinning him a line. His response was clear. 'Ah, right.'

CHAPTER ELEVEN

Create a show for the world with me
Make a special memory
Feel the romance of the choreography
Shine in the spotlight for all to see...

'These photos are great,' Dair said, seeing the previews of the pictures the photographer had taken. Huntine was included in several of them.

The photographer set up his camera ready to video the clips, and began with Dair playing his electric guitar and singing one of his new songs.

Huntine stood to the side, watching Dair play the guitar, and then the piano.

'Could you stand near the piano,' the photographer said to Huntine.

She went over and joined Dair, and held a music sheet as he sang and played a second song. And then the third song, capturing a sample of all three new songs.

'Great,' the photographer said, and then glanced at the dance floor. 'I'll film you dancing now.'

Dair put on a recording of one of his songs, and stepped on to the floor. The photographer filmed Dair dancing part of the opening choreography for his show.

'Now change the music and give me another routine.'

Dair did as he suggested, and every impressive move, spin and jump was captured in the clip.

'Could the two of you pair up now and dance around the floor,' the photographer said, stepping back so that he could video them.

Huntine hesitated. 'I'm not dancing in Dair's show.'

'Oh, I thought you were performing on the tour,' said the photographer.

'No, I'm not part of the show.'

'But Huntine is a wonderful dancer,' said Dair. He held his hand out to her. 'Come and waltz with me around the floor.'

Huntine let Dair take her in hold and they waltzed around to a romantic song while the photographer filmed them.

'Dance the tango routine with me,' Dair said to her as the music changed. 'The routine we danced at the studio.'

She needed little reminder of the tango as the steps, the choreography, was burned into her thoughts.

'Wonderful, keep going,' the photographer encouraged them while filming every moment.

When they finished, the photographer replayed the footage back to them.

Seeing herself dancing with Dair made her heart react. They danced well together.

Afterwards, the photographer packed up his equipment. 'I'll have these pics and clips ready for you later today,' he said to Dair. 'And I'll see you soon at the filming of your dance show. I'm one of the team your tour director has hired to make the video at the dance studio.'

'Great,' said Dair, and walked him out to his car.

Huntine wandered over to the piano, seeing the music sheets propped up, her lyrics written on them. Glancing around, she felt a surge of excitement mixed with realisation that the dance tour dates were closing in. Almost time for the dance video filming in the stage room at the studio. Nearly time for them to go their separate ways when the tour began. Her heart twisted as she looked around the living room, thinking that the fun times she'd had here with Dair were soon to be nothing more than happy memories.

Dair came bounding in and his energy swept away her doleful thoughts.

'That went well, better than I'd even hoped,' he said with a bright smile. 'Thank you for diving in and dancing with me. I know we hadn't planned or rehearsed it, but seeing the clips, our timing and styling was perfect.'

'Do you think Shona will be miffed? After all, she's your leading lady in the show.'

'No, Shona's part of the dancing, not the songwriting. These pictures and clips are to promote the songs and you as the lyric writer. Shona will shine when it comes to the dance show.'

Huntine smiled, and went to get ready to leave. They both had busy days ahead.

'Cup of tea before you go? Maybe a scone?'

She laughed, and followed him through to the kitchen.

'I'm going to coordinate the upload of the songs on to my website with my tour director later today,' Dair said while making the tea and buttering the scones.

'I'll send you a copy of the songs, and a link to the website when it goes live.'

'I'm keen to listen to the recordings.'

He cut the large soda scone in two and put it on a plate with the fruit scone.

Huntine picked up a soda scone half, leaving the other half and fruit scone for Dair.

While they were having their tea and scones, Cambeul phoned Huntine.

'Can we meet for dinner tonight?' said Cambeul. 'I'd like to chat about the play, organise a few things, including more publicity.'

'Dinner, yes, where?' she said.

'I'll book a table at our favourite restaurant.'

'I'll meet you there at seven, Cambeul.'

Dair washed down a mouthful of fruit scone, and the unwanted taste of jealousy, chiding himself for feeling like this. He knew Cambeul was waiting patiently in the wings for the right time to ask Huntine out on a real date. But Huntine seemed to have no romantic feelings towards Cambeul. And none that he could claim she'd showed for him either.

It was Huntine's turn to question Dair. 'Penny for your thoughts.'

'I'm thinking about updating my website with the songs. Selecting a cover picture. Making sure I credit you as the lyricist. My mind is buzzing with a to–do list.'

If she suspected he was wrapping the truth in plausible fibs, she showed no sign of it.

Instead, she smiled, finished her tea and the remnants of her soda scone. 'I'll let you get on with your busy day,' she said. Planning to push on with hers.

Dair walked her to her car and waved her off.

He then went up to his bedroom, changed out of his ghillie shirt and trews, put on casual training gear and set to work preparing the website for the songs.

Working through lunch and into the afternoon, he coordinated his plans for the presentation of the songs with his tour director. By the late afternoon, the photographer sent the pictures and video clips, allowing Dair and his director to select what they needed.

An amber twilight shone into the living room where Dair sat working at his laptop. Easing the tension from his shoulders, he finally finished the work. The songs were now available for purchase and download from his website.

Checking the time and seeing that it was just after seven, he sent a link to Huntine, and a few others, including Mullcairn.

Then he started making an easy dinner for himself using the groceries that Huntine had brought. He made scrambled eggs, grilled the two remaining slices of Lorne sausage, served with tomatoes, beans and bread and butter. Pudding was strawberries, raspberries and yoghurt.

He pictured Huntine would be having dinner with Cambeul as he tucked into his eggs and sausage. The video clips of her dancing replayed in his thoughts, and feelings of longing made him warn himself again not to fall in love with her.

Huntine sat opposite Cambeul having dinner at their favourite restaurant with a view of the city out the window. The lights of Edinburgh glittered in the distance, and she found herself thinking about Dair for a moment, and then blinking back to her conversation with Cambeul.

'...and all the costume fittings are finished, so we can have our next dress rehearsal as planned,' said Cambeul. 'Oh, and, ticket sales are doing well, especially with the recent publicity we've had. Will you be on the radio again? The Mullcairn show?'

'I'm not sure. I think Dair will be invited back on. He's working on adding the songs to his website today.' She told Cambeul about the photo–shoot.

'Pictures and video clips.' Cambeul sounded interested. 'Do you think we should add things like that to promote the play?'

'I do. The photographer was excellent. Maybe we could hire him. He's part of the team filming Dair's dance show in the studio room.'

'Get the photographer's number and I'll call him and get this organised.'

'He gave me his contact number.' She paused from eating her roast dinner and checked her phone. 'Yes, here it is.' As she sent it to Cambeul, she noticed she had a message from Dair. She read the message. 'Dair has sent me a link to his website. The songs are now live.'

'Give me the link. I'd like to hear the songs you've been working on.'

She sent Cambeul the link, and then they both couldn't resist viewing the pictures and the videos that were added to promote the music.

Cambeul downloaded the songs. 'Tell Dair I'm one of his first customers.'

'We can't play these in the restaurant,' she whispered to Cambeul.

'I just want to hear a whisper of what one of the songs sounds like.' Cambeul quietly played the first of the three songs, and they both listened for a minute before clicking the music off and continuing to eat their dinner.

'I'm more than a little bit impressed,' Cambeul enthused. 'And you know how fussy I am when it comes to music. The quality of the recording is excellent, and Dair's a fine singer. I don't know what I expected him to sound like, but he's far more tuneful than I thought he'd be. And I love your lyrics.'

'Thank you, Cambeul. I'll tell Dair.' She sent a message to Dair, and then finished her main course.

Cambeul browsed the menu. 'I'm tempted by the sticky toffee pudding.'

Huntine ordered the traditional Scottish trifle.

'I'm surprised that Dair kept his shirt on in all the photos,' Cambeul commented playfully as they ate their puddings.

Huntine giggled. 'Don't be a rascal, Cambeul.'

'I liked his ghillie shirt. I've actually got a shirt like that at home that I wear to ceilidh parties. But I tie my shirt laces.'

'You're the buttoned up type. Always well–dressed.'

Cambeul smiled at her and took the compliment.

Dair was finishing his pudding when a call came through from Mullcairn's radio show.

'Hello, Dair, I'm Mullcairn's assistant. Mullcairn received your message. He's been listening to your songs, and he'd like to do a phone–in interview with you on tonight's show. It's on at the moment, but would you be available in half an hour to chat live on air about your new songs?'

'Yes, I'd be happy to take part.'

'Again, it's short notice, but Mullcairn would like to have you and Huntine Grey as his guests tonight. Do you think Huntine could join us to chat about her song lyrics?'

'I'm sure she would. I'll call her and we'll be ready for the phone–in.'

'Wonderful, Dair. I'll tell Mullcairn. He'd like to play one or two of your songs during the show.'

After the call, Dair phoned Huntine.

'Mullcairn wants us to be phone–in guests on his radio show tonight in half an hour,' Dair told her. 'He's going to play the songs live on air. I know you're having dinner with Cambeul, but can you join in?'

'Yes, I'm at the restaurant, but we've finished dinner. I'll head home right now.'

'Or come here to my house. We can do the phone–in together.'

'Okay, I'm on my way.'

Cambeul surmised what was happening.

Huntine stood up. 'I have to go. Mullcairn is going to play the songs on the radio tonight.' She summarised the situation as he settled the bill and hurried with her to her car parked nearby.

'What time are you on?' said Cambeul. 'I want to tune–in.'

'In about half an hour.'

Dair welcomed Huntine when she arrived at his house. 'I thought we could sit in the living room for the phone–in.'

Huntine took her coat off, put her bag down and got her phone set up to make the call. She wore a white silk blouse and classy grey trousers, while he was wearing a vest and training trousers.

The kettle clicked off the boil in the kitchen and Dair hurried through. 'I'll make us a quick cup of tea. We'll be on in a few minutes.'

She settled down on the couch. 'Cambeul bought your songs,' she called through to Dair. 'He listened to snippets of your singing at the restaurant. He was really impressed.'

Dair came through with two mugs of tea and put them on the coffee table.

'I'm glad he liked the songs.' He sat down on the couch beside her.

'He's going to be listening in,' she added.

'My tour director is going to listen to the show, and I've messaged a few others that we're on tonight.'

Moments later, Dair and Huntine both received messages prompting them to phone the radio show.

'I thought we could use my phone on speaker for the call,' she said.

Huntine phoned in and they listened as Mullcairn introduced them to the listeners.

'*As promised, I have Dair and Huntine on the show this evening to talk about their new songs, released today as three new singles,*' Mullcairn announced, and gave a link to where the songs could be downloaded from Dair's website. '*Hello to you both, and welcome to the show.*'

'*Hello, Mullcairn,*' said Huntine.

'*Thanks for inviting us on the show tonight,*' Dair added.

'*Before we begin, I'm going to play one of the new songs,*' said Mullcairn. '*Dair is singing, playing the piano and guitar. He wrote the music, and Huntine Grey wrote the lyrics...*'

CHAPTER TWELVE

The passion of our dance
Lingers in the night
I'll remember this evening dancing
Wishing it was true romancing
Dance once more with me tonight...

'To play us out tonight, is another one of Dair and Huntine's new songs,' said Mullcairn. *'Remember, you heard them here first on tonight's show. Thanks for listening in. Join me, Mullcairn, again soon for another evening of cheery chatter and great music.'*

The song began to play, ending the radio interview.

After taking part in the radio show, Huntine turned her phone off and they relaxed back on the couch, happy that the interview had gone well.

Messages started to pop up on their phones from Cambeul, Huntine's grandmother, Dair's tour director and a few other acquaintances who'd tuned in to the show.

They replied to their messages and then turned their phones off to relax and unwind.

'Your songs sounded great listening to them played on the show,' said Huntine.

'Thanks to you for suggesting I record them.'

'Are you planning to write and record any other songs?'

'Not at the moment. I'm going to concentrate on the dance tour now. I can hardly believe it's getting so close to the launch date.'

'I feel the same about the play.'

'How's your novel writing going? I feel I'm taking up so much of your time.'

'I'm on schedule. Writing a lot late at night. But I'll have more time once the play opens and starts to tour.'

'And you won't have me distracting you,' he said, smiling.

'You are such a bad distraction,' she teased him.

Dair stood up and rolled away the tension he'd been holding in his shoulders during the radio show. 'Cup of tea before you go to start work on your book.'

'Yes, please. And I don't know that I'll write tonight. I'll decide later. But I got some writing done today between the chaos and your distractions.'

He spoke as he went through and filled the kettle for tea. 'Take the rest of the night off then,' he suggested.

Huntine relaxed back on the couch, feeling the tension unravel. 'I think I'll do that. I'll sleep on ideas for the next chapter and wake refreshed and ready to write in the morning.'

She heard him rattling around in the kitchen, and then he brought two mugs of tea through to the living room, handed one to her, and sat down on the couch.

'What are you planning to do?' she said, sipping her tea.

'Dance.'

'Working on the choreography?'

145

He nodded. 'Want to join me?' His lips curved into a warm smile. 'You're wearing your dancing shoes.'

'One routine, and then I'll head home,' she suggested.

Dair's face lit up with a smile and he went over and put some music on. 'How flexible are you?'

'What have I let myself in for?' she joked, standing up and getting ready to join him on the dance floor.

'On a scale of one to ten,' he prompted her. 'When we were dancing in the studio, I felt that you kept yourself very fit and limber.'

'I do my ballet stretches every day. I feel better after a ballet barre routine, and it only takes several minutes. It's something I've done for years, since I trained in ballet as a wee girl. And it helps when I've been sitting writing for hours to ease off the tension.'

'Ten then,' he assessed.

'Close enough. I don't really rate my ability to stretch. It's just something I do every day. I enjoy it.'

The music had an upbeat rhythm. 'This is one of the routines in Act Two. It starts with a wee bit of salsa.' He pulled her into hold and they started salsa dancing. 'Freestyle it. Let yourself go, feel the rhythm.'

Huntine did as he suggested, and they began to move to the beat of the song, an instrumental piece that then tailed off into a romantic tune before becoming dramatic.

'Will you let me lift you?' he said.

Huntine hesitated.

'I won't drop you, or spin you overhead, not unless you're okay with that.'

She searched his face for any sign that he was joking, and realised he wasn't.

'I'm doing a few combinations of lifts with Shona. I obviously can't practise these on my own here at home, so I usually work around those parts of the routines, and try to picture any variations of the choreography in my mind. Then I'll practise these with Shona at the dance studio.'

'Tell me the combination of lifts.'

'It starts with a lift where I do this.' Dair put his arm around Huntine's waist, lifted her up and spun her around as he did a full turn, and then gently put her down.

Huntine laughed, taken aback by his strength and how easily he lifted her.

'The second lift has another spinning motion and then I whirl you around in my arms.'

Without hesitation, Dair scooped Huntine up in his arms and she could feel the strength in him lift her with ease. Her feet barely touched the floor as he danced around with her.

Whenever Dair lifted her and held her in his arms, her heart reacted to his strong physique and dancing techniques, beating fast, sensing the romance in the choreography. It wasn't real romance, she reminded herself, just a show dance romance for the performance. Acting like a couple in love, portraying the dance characters.

'Now foxtrot with me,' said Dair.

They fell into step, matching each other's movements, and danced across the floor, adding flair and flamboyance to the foxtrot.

Huntine smiled as they skip–stepped around the floor as the music changed to an equally upbeat song.

'Now there's another lift,' he said, clasping her around the waist, lifting her as he turned.

Her fingers could feel the strength of his muscles, contrasting with the lightness of his dancing.

Their impromptu lifts made Huntine remember her skills from the past and she began to add her own flair to the routine, mainly through extending her arms to elongate the lines of their dance movements.

'Now cross step in front,' he instructed. 'And behind. Then repeat to the midway point of the song. We're almost halfway through the routine.'

While they danced, Dair added to the choreography. 'This is a variation I have in mind. I've not yet practised it with Shona.'

'It's impressive choreography, but can I suggest that the transition we've just done is lengthened to smooth out the changeover of the lifts with the lively choreography.'

'Let's try that,' he said, sounding up for her suggestion.

They ran through the routine again, and then paused as he changed the music.

'That was exhilarating,' said Huntine.

'Can we try again with a different song?' he hurried to change the music. 'This is my second choice of music for this routine.'

'Faster or slower?'

'Much faster. Something I think the audience will love to sing and clap along to.' Dair gazed down at her as they began in close hold. 'Freestyle any parts you wish. Raise the bar for this routine too.'

Huntine sensed the energy build in the song, and between her and Dair. Halfway through, something clicked in their continuity, and they became even more in sync with each other as they danced around the floor.

He felt her style was different to Shona's, but both had their merits. Huntine's balletic strength shone through, especially when it came to the extensions of the arms and legs in the lifts. Her abilities were less show dance and more romance. Huntine was such a classic dancer. But the show required a fine balance between the two. Poise and pizzazz. Entertaining the audience.

Huntine recalled some of the routine she'd watched at the dance studio when Dair was rehearsing with Shona.

Dair replayed the music, and they performed another run through of the routine. This time, Huntine danced with more flair and jazzed–up the steps between the lifts, using moves from her skills in modern stage training.

Matching her moves, Dair upped his performance, and he felt he'd added to the choreography and would incorporate this into the routine.

'Would you mind dancing part of the ceilidh routine with me from the opening number?' said Dair.

She was enjoying herself more than she'd anticipated, and didn't want their night of dancing to end, so she agreed to try the challenging ceilidh choreography.

Dair verbally ran through the first part of the routine, and Huntine nodded, knowing the pieces of the ceilidh dances he'd combined to create it. She loved ballet, but she loved ceilidh and Scottish Highland dancing too.

The music was rousing, and they got ready to step into the beat in time with each other, and whirled around the floor.

Huntine felt Dair's strength take charge of the dance, but she was familiar with the Scottish dances and she picked up her pace to equal his, adding an elegant edge to his vigorous routine.

The energy that ignited between them spurred them on, and by the time the song finished, Dair's heart was racing, not from exertion, but from exhilaration.

They looked at each other for a moment, and her heartbeat matched his, thundering with the passion of their dancing. How she missed this type of intensity that dancing could bring. She'd chosen the right career path with her writing, but dancing with a man like Dair, feeling herself pressed against his strong–beating heart, the power of his arms wrapped around her, was an experience she'd long remember.

Dair spun her around in a sequence of waist lifts in time to the lively, Scottish music. She felt the muscles in his arms and shoulders with every move.

He could barely contain the fire of desire burning in him as he danced with this beautiful woman. Of all the women he'd ever partnered with, Huntine was surely his perfect match.

The ceilidh dancing brought the best out of her, and he'd thought her ballet skills had been wonderful, but tonight the Scottish core of dancing raised the routine to an unforgettable level.

They finished in a dynamic move, facing each other, a lover's challenge in the story of this routine. And for a moment, he sensed that the challenge was real, that in other circumstances, they could be the lovers he'd created for the wild, romantic and rousing opening sequence to the show.

He held her for a moment and then reluctantly let her go, stepping back, sweeping his hair away from his brow. 'That was incredible,' he said, his breath ragged with hidden passion. She was incredible, he thought to himself.

Huntine smiled, her thoughts in a whirlwind, her resolve not to engage in a summer romance, cast to the wind. Needing a moment to gather herself, she tried to look happy while wondering if he knew the effect he had on her when they danced.

'At this rate, I'm going to have to credit you with helping me create the choreography, not just the song lyrics.'

She smiled again. 'No, the choreography is all yours. This was one of those times when everything comes together in a dance to create a special memory.'

'I'll certainly never forget this evening dancing here with you.' He couldn't have been more sure or sincere with his comment.

'It's been a wild night.' Her tone indicated that she was now going to get ready to head home. 'The radio show, dancing with you, ceilidh moves and being lifted.'

And their romantic dancing, he thought, wishing the night wasn't over, but knowing he had to let her go.

'I had fun dancing with you tonight,' she said as they stepped outside and he walked her to her car. 'Despite you being a bad influence on me, encouraging me to dance the night away when I should've been getting on with my writing, or getting a decent night's sleep.'

He gave her a mischievous smile. 'The fun outweighs my bad influence I hope.'

'It does.' She smiled back at him and got into her car and spoke to him through the open window. 'I'll see you when I see you.'

'You will.'

Huntine drove off, and he lingered for a moment, breathing in the mild evening air. Gazing up at the vast starry sky arching above him, he had a feeling of excitement, as if something was bubbling under the surface, a sense of something special.

Shrugging off the feeling, he went inside and sat in the living room, making notes of the new moves for the choreography.

Then checking his phone for messages before starting to get ready for bed, he blinked, seeing his phone light up with numerous missed calls. He'd turned his phone off earlier and hadn't switched it back on.

His tour director had been phoning and left several urgent messages. Dair realised the urgency when he listened to the first message. Sales of the music had soared, and people were contacting his director to ask about the songs.

Dair phoned his director, and was brought up to speed on the situation. They agreed to talk in the morning to see if the influx of sales slowed down overnight.

After the call, Dair checked his website. People had listened in to the radio show, liked the songs, and then downloaded them from his website.

Dair phoned Huntine, eager to tell her even though it was late at night. The chances were that she hadn't gone to bed and was still up writing.

Huntine picked up the call.

'People are downloading the songs from the website,' he said. 'They heard the songs played on the Mullcairn show. I'd turned my phone off, so I've only just found out that the sales have really taken off.'

'That's wonderful!'

'My tour director and I are going to chat in the morning. Sales could slow down overnight, but what a great start. People have left messages too, saying they love the songs.'

'I'm so pleased,' she said.

'Are you working late writing your book?'

'Oh, yes.'

He laughed. 'I'll let you get on. I'll phone you tomorrow with any updates on the song sales.'

'Do that. Goodnight, Dair.'

'It certainly has been,' he said.

After the call, Huntine continued writing for another hour, sitting typing at her laptop with a view of the city. Edinburgh wore the night well, she thought. The wonderful architecture was silhouetted against the dark sky, and the vibrant energy rose up in layers of lights, from the winding streets to the windows aglow. Every night since she'd been there told a different story. Sometimes the city was buzzing with activity, and she sensed the nightlife, people dining at the restaurants, enjoying a night out dancing or at the theatre. And other times a rainy night atmosphere draped itself over everything creating a tale of cosy evenings inside snuggled by the fire. But tonight, she sensed a story of excitement bubbling under the starry sky.

Taking a sip of her tea, she continued to write her book. The events of the evening, starting with dinner at the restaurant with Cambeul, then the interview on the Mullcairn radio show, followed by a wild night of dancing with Dair, had filled her with ideas for her novel. Romance and drama.

Her fingers moved at speed over the keys, touch typing, often glancing out the window at the city. When she'd first moved to Edinburgh, temporarily to work with Cambeul on the play, she hadn't anticipated getting involved with Dair and his dancing and music.

Dair took a shower and went to bed, expecting he'd hardly be able to sleep for the unexpected news about the songs. Instead, he fell asleep soundly and woke up to a lovely bright morning that looked like summer.

But he'd been busy in his dreams, dancing with Huntine, lifting her up in energetic moves, spinning around a dreamlike stage lit with dazzling lights.

By the time he padded through to the kitchen in his silk boxers to make breakfast, he felt that he'd already had a full dancing workout.

While the kettle boiled he made toast, and opened the kitchen door wide to let the morning air in while he sat at the table pondering the busy day ahead. He'd deliberately not checked his phone for messages yet, or the song sales, until after he'd had sustenance, knowing he'd need to be ready to tackle the workload.

After he finished his toast, he stood cupping his mug of tea at the kitchen door, looking out into the back garden where the spring flowers now had a colourful chorus of summer blooms.

And the steady beat of his heart quickened, sensing the time drawing in until the tour took him on a whirlwind adventure of a lifetime to the cities, towns, villages and islands throughout Scotland.

Gulping down the remainder of his tea, he checked his website. His eyes widened when he saw that the sales hadn't tailed–off overnight. The song section was buzzing with activity. Now it was time for him to do the same.

Huntine sat in the kitchen of her flat eating a bowl of porridge. Her laptop was set up on the kitchen table. She often did this after writing late into the night, and read over what she'd written with a fresh eye in the morning at breakfast.

But as the sunlight poured through the window, casting a warm glow across the little kitchen, she checked Dair's website. She couldn't see the details of his sales, but she could certainly see the numerous messages people had left for him, saying they loved the songs.

Smiling to herself, she clicked his website off. Taking her laptop through to the living room, she set it up near the window. Edinburgh looked like it was wearing summer this morning and had cast spring aside.

Then she started to write the next part of her novel. She had a stock of groceries in, no need to venture out, and planned a cosy and productive writing day, snuggled up, away from the busy outside world.

CHAPTER THIRTEEN

Let me wrap my arms around you
And take you in hold
I want to dance with you all evening
Never let you go...

The lights from the windows of the cafes, bars and restaurants shone on to the Edinburgh streets as Huntine walked along, heading to the dance studio. Cobbled niches trickled off from the main thoroughfare, leading to other popular eateries and entertainment venues.

The night had a warmth to it, and she wore her coat unbuttoned over her classic black trousers and grey silk blouse. Her hair hung in waves to her shoulders, and she'd added a touch more makeup for an evening look.

The photographer that Cambeul had hired smiled at Huntine when she arrived at the stage room where he was taking pictures of the actors during the photo–shoot.

The actors were in full costume and makeup, ready to perform a dress rehearsal of the play. The atmospheric lighting already created a sense of a bygone era, set in the heart of Edinburgh past. The vintage costumes were pre–loved, redesigned to enjoy another outing on stage and add to the romanticism of the play. A stylised version of reality, the traditional costume designs comprised of classic suits and dresses.

The scenery depicted an old–fashioned shop set in a street lit with lanterns. A cityscape from yesteryear was backlit to add depth to the romantic drama, particularly in Act One.

Cambeul darted around, clasping a copy of the script, organising the actors, coordinating the lighting and sound with the crew, and looking anxiously around hoping Huntine would arrive soon. Impeccably dressed in a three–piece suit, he breathed a sigh of relief when he saw her walk in.

He hurried towards her. 'I thought you'd forgotten or mixed up the dates.'

'Have I ever done that?' Huntine said calmly.

'No, but there's always a first time. I messaged you, twice.'

'I replied, twice.'

'I didn't get your messages,' he complained, and checked his phone. 'There are no—oh, yes, here they are. I've been in such a tizzy I didn't notice them. Sorry.'

Huntine shrugged off her coat and put it down on the seat where she planned to watch the performance. It was further back than previous nights when she'd sat beside Cambeul during rehearsals. The stage room wasn't a theatre per se, but chairs had been set up by the dance studio staff to seat Huntine, Cambeul, and a handful of select guests who were already settled and awaiting the performance.

'The stage looks great,' Huntine commented.

'It's magnificent,' Cambeul enthused. 'The amber lights that we added to the blue for the opening scene create the feeling of Edinburgh in bygone times. At night, with mischief and romance bubbling under the surface. Our leading man will stand under the glow of a lamp in the cobbled street, gazing out into the night, wondering...will I ever see her again? The only woman he ever truly loved.'

'You've been reading the dialogue again,' she teased him.

'Even in my sleep,' he said, smiling. 'And I'm not joking. But you know what I'm like when we get closer to the opening of a play.'

'You wind yourself up too tight. Then you unravel at speed.' She smiled reassuringly. 'The plays have gone well so far. There might be moments that aren't quite perfect, but the audience don't have your level of nit–pickingness. If that's even a word.'

'You should know. You're the wordsmith.'

'Then I'm unofficially adding it to our vocabulary, Cambeul.'

He frowned and wrung the script in his hands.

'Stop fussing,' she insisted. 'This is just the dress rehearsal. And the photographer seems to have everything in hand for taking the pictures and video clips.'

'Ah, a slight change of plan regarding the latter,' Cambeul confessed.

She'd seen that look before when he'd meddled with things without talking them through with her.

'You've been so busy with the radio interviews, the song lyrics, dancing with Dair,' he reasoned.

'I should never have told you about him lifting me.'

159

'It sounded entertaining. Maybe we'll put lifts into the ballroom dance choreography for the Christmas play. How is that going by the way? Have you had time to enhance the dialogue in the opening act? Make it more Christmassy and romantic?'

'Yes, and I've whizzed a copy off to the theatre producer so he can have a read at it.'

'We're in for a whirlwind of a year,' said Cambeul, looking like he was already in the eye of it. 'First the sensational summer play tour, then rustling up another romantic drama play for the autumn, and creating a hat trick of entertainment with a festive Christmas finale that includes ballroom dancing — and lifts.'

'We should use that comment on the publicity material. It pretty much sums things up, and makes them sound feasible.'

Then she noticed that the actors were really buzzing around the stage area. 'The actors seem extra excited,' she assessed. 'The way they look when they're about to perform live for an audience.' Something in her jarred, and she immediately glanced round to check that there wasn't an audience. There was no one out of the ordinary. Just the usual assistants and friends who were keen to see the full dress rehearsal.

Cambeul footered with his script and looked guilty.

'What have you done?' Huntine's tone was edged with suspicion.

Cambeul feigned a smile. 'You know we had been discussing the idea of making a video of the play,' he began. 'When I phoned the photographer, using the number you gave me, I booked him to come along this evening and take some pictures and a few highlight clips of the play. But he offered to film the whole performance for very little extra cost and kerfuffle.'

Huntine blinked as the situation became clear. 'You've hired the photographer to make a full video of the play.'

'That sums it up succinctly.'

'Embellish with the details,' she prompted him.

'Well, he's brought one of his colleagues, a videographer, with him. They both have cameras that will focus on the whole stage and provide close–ups of the actors performing. And they assure me the sound quality is excellent. The cameras and equipment these days enables them to create what we need. After the play's tour, we can make the video available for download.' Cambeul took a deep breath. 'What do you think? Great idea or not?'

'I think you should've told me,' she scolded him, while liking the idea.

'Sorry, sorry...'

The lights changed as the atmosphere on the stage was being created ready for the start of the performance.

'Curtain up in ten minutes,' one of the stage crew announced.

The photographer came hurrying over to Huntine and Cambeul. 'We're all set up. The lighting in here is perfect. Atmospheric, but with enough ambiance to add to the quality of the video.'

'Is there anything I need to do during the performance?' Cambeul said to the photographer.

'Sit without fidgeting while you watch the play from further back,' the photographer told him. 'No offence, you're obviously anxious about the performance, but a jackrabbit in the front row would be a distraction. It's easier to have you out of the frame rather than try to edit you out for the finished video.'

Cambeul nodded, agreeing with the photographer's suggestion.

'Is your play touring like Dair's dance show?' The photographer said to Huntine. 'Are you touring on the same circuit of theatres throughout Scotland?'

'We sometimes use the same theatres, but Dair's show is a whirlwind of one or two night performances per venue in each city and town. Whereas, the play has a week to ten days run at each theatre, with lots of matinee performances too.'

'So, you're staying longer in each city or town,' the photographer wanted to clarify.

'Yes,' said Huntine. 'But I won't be touring with the show. I'll attend the opening night in Edinburgh, and perhaps an evening in Glasgow. Cambeul will be touring with the play.'

The photographer nodded that he understood, and then adjusted his camera. 'I'll take pics during the show. But can I get a picture of the two of you with the stage in the background, for context, before the play starts?'

Huntine and Cambeul manoeuvred themselves so that the picture could be taken to include the stage.

The photographer checked the image. 'Superb.' Then he hurried away to talk to the videographer as the play was about to start.

Cambeul sat beside Huntine, and she took his copy of the script off him rather than put up with his perpetual fidgeting with it.

'Sorry, Huntine,' Cambeul whispered as a hush fell over the audience of acquaintances. 'Oh, and I was going to invite Dair and his dancers to join us, but it seems they're deep in learning new choreography this evening.'

Huntine had lost track of Dair's schedule. 'Is he rehearsing his choreography tonight in the dance room?'

'He is. But no one is allowed to even have a peek in here while the play is on. There's a notice pinned to the door telling people not to come in.'

Dair practised the new lifts with Shona.

'I prefer these lifts,' she said to him. 'They flow better with the choreography. I like your new ideas.'

A pang of guilt shot through him. These were Huntine's ideas when she'd danced with him recently. The night he'd thrown her around his living room like a rag doll, and she hadn't complained. Instead, she'd suggested the variations that Shona had just danced with him.

Dair was still thinking about this when Shona's voice jarred his faraway thoughts.

'I don't know if I've mentioned, but congratulations on the soaring sales of your new songs.'

'Thanks, Shona.'

'The songs are great to dance to,' she said. 'I think the reason is that they were written by a dancer.'

He blinked, surprised by her assessment, but agreeing with her because he always danced to the songs he was writing, trying out the rhythm.

'We know that some songs are great to listen to, and in theory they should be ideal for dancing to,' she said. 'But that's not the case. A beat can be a bit off for dance routines, an awkward change of rhythm midway through the song, often as the chorus starts. Your songs hit all the right notes for dancing, whether it's fast–paced, upbeat or a slow dance number.'

Dair thanked her again, realising this was why he'd partnered with Shona years ago. She thought deeply about dancing, and rarely sugared the pill when he wanted her opinion on his performances. This was during their time competing on the dance circuits, and before he'd created his own show. They'd been invited to take part in shows, backing the lead dancers. And that's where he'd found his love of dance tours. Now he had his own tour, and was glad that Shona was part of it.

'You're frowning,' Shona told him. 'Stop being a worry wart.'

Dair smiled. 'I was just thinking about the past.'

'Well don't. You'll give yourself frown lines. And worse, you'll give them to me too.'

Smiling, Dair played the music. 'Let's run through the lifts again,' he said to Shona.

The three other dance couples joined in and they all practised the sequences several times until the timing was perfect.

Dair watched them in the mirror, picturing the dance performance on stage with atmospheric lighting, and knew they'd created something special.

'Can we go over the mid–point of the routine for Act Two?' one of the men said to Dair.

'Yes.' Dair changed the music, and they stepped right into the routine. It comprised of a combination of lifts. Staccato moves were included in this part of the choreography, performed with sharp, dynamic bursts of energy.

All of them were in their element, expressing the music with distinct steps and powerful interaction with each other.

'Excellent,' Dair said when they finished. Then they practised it again.

Dair could see the joy on all their faces, loving rehearsals like this when the air was charged with energy, and they danced together in one mesmerising performance.

When they finished, they gave an involuntary round of applause, high–fives to each other and broad smiles.

Moments like this were the essence of dance, Dair thought to himself. He wished he could bottle that essence. Their shared love of dancing shone through any tiredness they might have felt after the arduous rehearsals.

Ensconced in her own world of theatre, Huntine watched the play unfold.

Each act outshone the next, in her opinion, though the looks that Cambeul gave her as they sat together watching the performance, showed that he was as impressed as her.

'The actors have really pulled it out of the bag tonight,' Cambeul whispered to her.

'I'm glad it's being videoed,' she whispered back. She flicked a glance towards the photographer and the videographer filming every entertaining moment.

CHAPTER FOURTEEN

Under a starry sky
Waltz with me
To the rhythm of our song
They say our love will never last
I know we'll prove them wrong
Waltz with me my love
To the tune of our own sweet song...

'We'll have the video edited and ready for you soon,' the photographer said to Cambeul and Huntine after the play's full performance finished. He'd also taken pictures of Huntine and Cambeul standing on the stage with the full cast at the end of the show. 'And I'll send you the pictures and the video clips you wanted to promote the play on the website.'

Cambeul walked them out of the stage room, leaving Huntine to chat to the performers.

'When will you be auditioning for roles in your new autumn play?' one of the actors said to Huntine.

'There's gossip circulating that you're writing a festive Christmas play,' another actor added.

Huntine didn't want to get their hopes up too soon, or dash them either. She told them the situation.

'The recent publicity I've received, initially about the current play, and then for writing the lyrics for Dair's songs, changed some of my plans. Including my plans to work with Cambeul on my next play, and my back–burner Christmas play. The short–course is this — I'm going to finish writing my novel, and start

167

writing my next play which will be another romantic drama, set in the past. I've some of it mapped out, and Cambeul will direct it. If we can get our act together, it'll launch in the autumn as the current play finishes in the summer.'

The actors nodded, listening to the details of the play.

'We'll be auditioning for the autumn play soon, and hope to include many of you to work with us again,' Huntine added. 'But I know some of you have other projects lined up for the autumn.'

A few spoke up about this, but were eager to know about the Christmas show.

'A theatre producer has approached me,' Huntine continued. 'He's reading a Christmas play I'd written a wee while ago, and he's interested in it. Cambeul will direct it. There are ballroom dancing and stage dance routines in the story, and Cambeul and I will select a handful of actors with dancing skills for those roles. Cambeul will keep you all updated during the tour.'

The actors looked interested and were pleased with this news.

Cambeul came back in and joined the chatter.

'I'm going to head home now and get some more of my novel written,' Huntine confided to Cambeul.

He smiled and nodded.

Huntine put her coat on and headed out. The door to the dance room was open, but the lights were off, and she surmised that Dair's rehearsal evening had finished.

Walking out into the night, she buttoned up her coat. The air had a crispness to it as she walked to her car.

'How did the performance go?' a man's voice called to her.

She turned to see Dair hurrying to catch up with her. He wore his casual dance training gear and his bag was shrugged up on his shoulder.

'Great. It was a wonderful show. Everyone performed so well. Cambeul had organised a full video to be made.' She explained the details. 'We're confident the video will be a top–notch version of the play. But we won't make it available until after the tour is finished.'

'And the filming of it? Anything I should keep in mind when they video our dance show?'

There was so much she wanted to tell him, but standing in the street didn't seem the right place to chat. She glanced along towards the eatery that had the piano in it where they'd had their photographs taken for the press interview.

'Buy me a cup of tea, and I'll tell you everything that happened,' she said.

'Are you sure you've got time? I don't want to disrupt your plans.'

Huntine shrugged. 'It's fine, besides, I could do with a cup of tea.'

'And a bite of supper?' he added enticingly.

'Play the piano for me too?'

Dair's smile lit up his face, and they walked along to the eatery.

It was busy, but a couple were just leaving, and Dair and Huntine sat down at the vacant table that was next to the piano. No one was playing.

The special menu offered a tasty selection of savoury samples ranging from cheese, bread, butter, scones, mini sausage rolls, cheese pastries, pickles, relishes and salad.

They both ordered the special and a pot of tea for two.

Dair poured their tea, and they chatted while enjoying their supper. He picked up a sausage roll and listened as Huntine told him about the filming. 'They handled it well, and from the snippets that they showed me on the previews, they've captured the essence of the atmosphere. The whole stage, parts of it when the actors were highlighted front of stage, and close–ups.'

Dair looked bolstered by what she was telling him.

'I think they'll handle the filming of your dance show well too,' she said.

'Did you pause for a break or to reshoot parts of the play?'

'Only for a short break during the scheduled interval time. But no reshoots. The performances were excellent. It was one of those nights when everything went well. The atmosphere was fantastic.'

'It sounds like you've got a winning play,' he assessed.

'Watching it from start to finish really boosted my hopes that the tour will be successful. We have a great team of people, and we're all pulling together to make it work. I'm sure it's the same with you and your dancers.'

'It is,' he said. 'During tours and shows you create strong bonds of friendship.'

'We're both fortunate to do what we do.'

Dair agreed.

Huntine helped herself to a cheese pastry, and so did Dair.

She glanced at the piano, and then at the busy eatery. 'I thought someone would be tempted to play the piano.'

'Is that a less than subtle hint that you want me to play?'

'After you've finished having your supper.'

Dair gulped down a mouthful of his tea and stood up. 'Don't eat all the scones. I'll be back for mine after this song...'

Huntine smiled. 'What are you going to play?' she said as he sat at the piano.

'Something I wrote a while ago that I never finished.'

'Why didn't you finish it?'

'I don't know.' He sounded thoughtful. 'I just never sensed I had the right feeling for the chorus, or the last verse.' Starting to play the opening notes, he smiled over at her, and then concentrated on the song.

A beautiful melody rose up and Huntine sat calmly listening. It had a romantic element, and she noticed several people stopped from their lively chatter to watch Dair play. No one seemed to recognise him, and that made it all the more special, seeing their reaction to his song.

Having worked with him on his lyrics, she noticed where words were missing. Rather than bridge the gaps with his usual la la la fillers, he let the music speak for itself. Huntine was sure that most people listening didn't realise parts were missing, as his playing elevated the song.

She realised too, the effect his playing had on people as they quietened down to hear him.

At first, she thought the theme of the song was unrequited love, then she noted it was about wanting to find love, someone to share his world with.

As he glanced over at her, playing the last few notes, her heart fluttered from the feelings he stirred in her. His song exposed the inner longings of his own heart, and when he finished playing, those listening burst into applause.

Dair stood up, smiled acknowledgement and then sat down again opposite Huntine as the watermark returned to its lively social level again.

'That was a beautiful song,' Huntine told him.

'Maybe one day I'll finish it.' He took a sip of his tea.

'You should.'

He glanced over the rim of his cup at her. 'Lyrics are missing.'

'Is that a less than subtle hint that you want me to help you write them? Because I will, if you want. But hearing what you've written so far, and the melody, I think it would be better if you wrote them yourself, from the heart.'

He nodded, and picked up a scone and started to butter it. 'I've matured since I first started writing it.

There are things in my life that I love, especially my dancing, and my music. But I'm starting to feel as if there's something missing, a sense of wanting to settle down, even though my career is a whirlwind of touring. Do you ever feel like that?'

'I do. My writing allows me to tuck myself away for large parts of the year, so that's settling, and I love that. I enjoy feeling cosy at home, snuggled up, writing my novels and plays. Then there are pockets of activity, like being here in Edinburgh for the play's rehearsals with Cambeul. We keep in touch by phone, and messages as the play's script is ready, but then I have to pop over to Edinburgh to work with him until the opening night.'

'Then you go home again.'

'Yes, so there's a rhythm to the year, at least for the past few years. And I have to chat with my editor and publishers, and meet with them for the book launches and publicity. But those are sparks of activity in an otherwise quiet schedule, tucked away, writing, being the wordsmith.'

'Does it ever get lonely, writing on your own?'

She gave a thoughtful sigh. 'Not really, because there's never enough time for the writing, even when I seem ensconced at home thinking that I have weeks to relax and work on my books or scripts, all of a sudden the time whizzes by and suddenly there's a deadline looming. And I'm off to the races again, writing to meet the next deadline.' She smiled. 'For someone who spends so much time on my own, I'm incredibly busy.'

'Too busy to feel lonely,' he assessed.

'Yes, but that doesn't mean that I wouldn't like to be settled, in the romantic sense. I have tried, but clearly I've been unlucky.'

'That makes two of us,' he admitted.

'Maybe that's why we get along. Two fools when it comes to love. But creatively successful.'

'Excuse me,' a woman said to Dair. 'Are you the songwriting dancer?'

He smiled and nodded, still feeling unsure of such a title.

'I heard your music on the Mullcairn show.' She gestured to her table of friends. 'A few of us bought your songs. Was that a new song you were playing? It sounded lovely.'

'It's one that I'm working on,' Dair explained.

'I hope you finish it,' she said. And then she glanced over at her friends. 'We were wondering if you'd play one of your new songs.' She looked hopeful at him.

'Certainly.' Dair stood up and sat down at the piano and began to sing and play.

Huntine was happy to sit sipping her tea, wrapped in her cloak of invisibility as their respective roles in the world played out in real time.

The entire eatery seemed to pause while Dair played, and Huntine realised she had a glimpse of what was coming. Dair's career and popularity was due to soar. The man who was ready to settle down was about to be spotlighted from all angles. There would be no settling, certainly not this summer during his dazzling dance tour.

The beat of her own world was quickening, especially with the recent plans for a play for the autumn and the Christmas show. Plus, she might catch a few sparks from writing the lyrics for Dair's songs. She pictured nothing but the spotlight's glare for both of them, with Dair at the forefront. And a jarring surge of emotions charged through her. Success brought its own rewards, but it usually came at a cost. Would there even be time for them to be friends? Or would they drift, as people often do? This thought tore through her heart. She liked Dair. In other circumstances, he was a man she could easily fall in love with. And that acknowledgment in itself was hard to reconcile.

Dair finished playing the song, but then several people wanted their photo taken with him, and he cheerfully obliged before sitting back down with Huntine.

'I think we should skedaddle,' he said to Huntine, keeping his voice down.

Huntine nodded.

'I'll settle the bill.' He quickly paid while Huntine put her coat on and they made a hasty exit.

'I'm parked along here.' Huntine gestured ahead.

Dair walked with her and commented on what had happened. 'That was a wee bit wild.'

'A taste of things to come for you.'

'For us, surely.'

'You were the one singing and playing the piano. I got to finish the scones.'

He laughed.

They reached her car. 'Thanks for supper,' she said as she got in. 'And for letting me hear your unfinished melody.'

He nodded, and then gestured nearby. 'I'm parked over there.' He started to head to his car. 'See you at the dance show filming?'

'I'll be there, and so will Cambeul.'

Dair lifted his arm in acknowledgement as he walked away.

Huntine saw the headlights of Dair's silver car glint behind her as she drove off.

They drove in tandem along the main route out of the heart of the city, and then their cars peeled off in different directions as they both headed home.

Huntine decided not to watch the clock when she got back to her flat. Setting up her laptop at the window, she began writing her book where she'd left off while the view of Edinburgh told another nightly story.

Dramatic dark clouds scudded across the night sky, threatening a storm was brewing. The rainy atmosphere draped itself over the silhouettes of the buildings in the distance. Rain hit off the window, sparkling like fairy diamonds highlighted on the glass, and the pattering of it provided a descant to her typing as she worked on her writing before heading to bed.

CHAPTER FIFTEEN

This is the night where I dance with you
Holding you close to my heart
Though we're going separate ways
I never want to part
I'm holding you close to me
Close to my heart
I believe we'll be together
Somewhere down the line
When I'll be yours and you'll be mine...

The stage room was set ready for the filming of Dair's dance show, and buzzing with activity. An upright piano had been wheeled to the left of the stage for Dair to play, and his two guitars were on stands nearby. Lighting created the stage atmosphere in a triumphant glow of colourful starlike beams and dazzling spotlights.

For the opening of the show, the lights would be dimmed to shades of misty blue and rich heather purples as Dair played the piano, then guitar, while the dancers performed the ceilidh and modern dance routine. Then Dair would join them in the spectacular opening number.

Hair and makeup artists busied themselves, adding the finishing touches to the dancers' look for the show. Everyone was in costume, and changes in costume hung on rails backstage.

The dancers chatted excitedly, and although there was a level of nervousness, the pressure was eased knowing they weren't performing to a theatre audience, just a scattering of guests invited to sit and enjoy the show while it was being filmed. Any missteps could be rewound and performed again. Though all of them intended doing it right first time.

Dair wore his ghillie shirt and trews as he sat at the piano, tuning up, and going over the sequence of music and choreography in his mind. He could feel the adrenalin already kicking in.

Glancing at the door, he kept a lookout for Huntine arriving. Cambeul and other guests were already there. Moments later, he saw her arrive on time, looking lovely in a vintage tea dress and carrying her coat.

Jumping down from the stage, Dair hurried towards her, relieving her of the coat, and forcing himself not to give her a welcoming hug in front of everyone in case it was misinterpreted.

She'd anticipated he'd look handsome in his costume and stage makeup, but her heart wasn't ready for the feelings he ignited in her. His tall, broad–shouldered figure suited his costume. The laces of his ghillie shirt were tantalisingly undone to expose his lean–muscled chest, which given their height difference, was so near that she had an unrestricted close–up. The potency of his masculinity was turned up to a ten. Probably an eleven tonight. Her feelings towards him were off the scale.

Those fabulous turquoise eyes of his, emphasised to dramatic effect by the stage makeup, gazed down at her. It was clear that he was pleased to see her, and she didn't need a hug to feel the strength of his welcome.

'I've reserved a seat for you next to Cambeul.' Dair led her over to it and put her coat down.

'The stage looks amazing.' And so did Dair, but she kept this thought to herself. Her heart was fluttering wildly, and there was every chance she'd say something inappropriate such as how devastatingly sexy and gorgeous he was. She needed to settle her senses, like wading into a freezing cold sea and gradually becoming accustomed to the temperature. Though cold wasn't on offer this evening. She could feel a blush threaten to give away her reaction to him.

So she was relieved to see a distraction. Across the room, lit by the glow from the stage spotlights, Shona appeared to be chatting animatedly with Cambeul.

Dair followed Huntine's surprised eyeline and saw Cambeul and Shona.

Cambeul looked immaculate, wearing a classic pinstripe shirt, tie, and waistcoat. Shona's high–cut, purple–blue dress attested to the costume designer's lavish addition of glittery sequins to the chiffon and silk.

'When did those two become friends?' Huntine sounded as if she'd missed this unexpected event.

'I don't know.' Dair studied them. 'I wonder what they're talking about?'

'You're so buttoned–up, Cambeul!' Shona rebuked him. 'You'd be fairly fanciable if you weren't so...' She ran her hands through the front of his well–styled hair, ruffling it.

Huntine gasped. 'Did Shona just ruffle Cambeul's hair?'

'She doesn't even dare do that with mine,' Dair commented, wondering what was going on between them.

Huntine recoiled on the stage director's behalf. 'Cambeul won't like that. He'll have his comb out in a second.'

Several seconds ticked by without any comb being revealed.

Huntine looked at Dair for some sort of explanation. He had none. They continued to watch the interplay.

'Take your tie off,' Shona told Cambeul.

'I don't want to appear untidy,' he said.

'You're wearing a classy pinstripe shirt and waistcoat. No one could imagine you were unkempt,' she retorted.

Cambeul hesitated.

'Take it off, Cambeul!' said Shona.

Cambeul fumbled quickly to take his tie off. He rolled it up neatly and tucked it into his trouser pocket. 'Better?'

'Yes, but...' Shona leaned back to view him, still not satisfied with his makeshift makeover. 'Unbutton your collar.'

Cambeul looked aghast. 'I'm not baring my chest to all and sundry. I'm not Dair.'

'No, you're not, thankfully.'

Cambeul blinked. Was that an unintentional compliment?

Shona's blue eyes, accentuated by the dramatic stage makeup, stared at him. 'Undo the top two buttons.'

Realising he was on the losing end of the debate, Cambeul unbuttoned them.

Shona's elegant fingers ran along his collar, pleased with his new look. 'Suave but sexy.'

Cambeul had never had those words used to describe him before. He found he rather liked them.

'On in ten minutes!' Dair's tour director called to the dancers from his position on the stage, helping to organise everything.

'I'd better go and start getting ready for the show,' Dair said to Huntine. 'Tell me later if Shona manages to remove any other items of clothing from Cambeul.'

Huntine smiled. 'I will.'

Dair hurried away and jumped up on to the stage taking the short route up, and began talking to the tour director and other dancers, except Shona. She was still chatting to Cambeul.

Huntine watched Shona fuss some more with Cambeul. He appeared to be talking about his abdominals, patting his tummy.

'If I could get you down on the floor on a regular basis, Cambeul, I wouldn't be long in doubling your three–pack,' Shona said with assurance.

Cambeul guffawed.

'On one of my exercise mats,' Shona clarified.

'You have more than one?'

'I've got three. One for home, and two for touring. A spare one on tour in case I misplace one of my mats.'

'You certainly look spry,' he said.

'I'm very flexible.' Shona bent backwards while extending one leg high in the air.

'Shona!' the tour director shouted down to her and tapped his wrist.

'I have to go and warm–up,' she said to Cambeul. 'I expect to hear you cheering and clapping when I do anything exceptional on stage tonight.'

'The photographer told me that he didn't want me to make any sudden noises as they'd have to edit them out,' Cambeul told her.

Shona stared him down.

'But, stuff that,' Cambeul said, feeling freer. 'I'll be cheering you on, Shona.'

'That's what friends are for,' she said, and then skip–stepped away and joined the other dancers on stage.

Cambeul wandered over to Huntine, seeing the questioning looks she was giving him.

'I know what you're thinking, Huntine,' he said.

'I doubt it. But I am a bit surprised that you've become friends with Shona.'

'We met in the corridor, during our rehearsal nights here at the dance studio,' he started to explain. 'One evening we got chatting about her love of dancing, and she showed me her pirouettes. She's an incredible dancer.'

'Shona will be giving you dancing lessons next.'

'Oh, yes, she says she's eager to get me to take her in hold,' Cambeul agreed.

'You'll be waltzing around the dance floor soon.'

'No, Shona thinks she'd like to throw me right into a samba bouncing action. It sounds quite invigorating.'

'I'm glad you've become friends,' said Huntine.

'We've recently started to phone each other of an evening to chat. Shona tells me what she's been up to, and what I shouldn't be up to. It's well–balanced that way.'

Huntine bit back any comments.

'Unlike your enviably stoic one–word retorts, Huntine. Shona's verbosity is both impressive and strangely soothing. I now understand why you let me ramble on, while you remain quiet and listen to me babbling. It's surprisingly relaxing.'

Huntine smiled tightly.

'Now,' Cambeul said rather too loudly, 'when I want to relax, all I have to do is turn Shona on.'

The looks from those who'd overheard were entertaining.

Unaware of the entertainment and gossipmonger value of his comment, Cambeul added, 'It's like turning on the radio and tuning into your favourite show. And we like the same music. Shona's dance training since she was a wee girl has given her a compendium of classical music knowledge.'

'On in two minutes,' the tour director shouted.

Backstage, Dair and the dancers huddled in a group hug. Then as the lights dimmed, Dair hurried over and picked up his electric guitar, and the dancers took their places ready for the show to begin.

Huntine exchanged a glance with Cambeul as the audience lights dimmed and the stage lights shone, illuminating the dancers in a blue and purple glow, and the main spotlights were on Dair.

A second's pause, and then Dair began to play the opening riff of the first song on his electric guitar.

The sound in the studio room was particularly effective and the notes resonated out towards the small audience, and were picked up by the photographer and videographer filming every moment.

As the last note of the riff hung in the air, Dair quickly put the guitar aside, sat down at the piano and started to play and sing the song. The spotlights shone down on him.

Even though Huntine had heard it before, the effect of him singing and playing was strong and touched her heart in so many ways.

The song's outro finally led into the opening dance sequence where the dancers appeared from the glow of the lights and performed a mix of ceilidh dancing and modern stage to a popular song.

Dair joined them as the next song played, and they all danced the spectacular opening number. Performing individually, and as couples, the routine intertwined their talents. Shona was partnered with Dair, and the two of them looked like a perfect match as they spun around the floor.

This was followed by part of a Scottish sword dance performed by Dair. Then they all continued to perform the group dance.

Dazzling lights enhanced the dramatic dancing, and the air felt charged with the energy of the performance.

Huntine was enthralled, as was Cambeul and the others watching the show. The combination of popular dance styles including ballroom, Latin, ceilidh and Scottish dancing created an entertaining evening. As promised, Dair, wearing a kilt, performed a Highland Fling.

Just watching Dair made Huntine want to get up and dance. The tickets had been arranged for her grandparents to attend the dance show one night in Glasgow, and Huntine was sure they'd love it.

'Shona is an excellent dance partner for Dair,' Cambeul whispered to Huntine.

'She is.' Huntine recognised the lift routine, watching Dair dance with Shona.

'Are these some of the lifts you were dancing with Dair?' Cambeul whispered to her.

She nodded. 'I think they work.'

'They do,' Cambeul agreed, admiring Shona's performance and clapping loudly when she danced any special moves.

A brief interval was followed by a spectacular sequence of dances, with efficient costume changes, and no mistakes, at least on the surface. Nothing needed filmed again. Everyone danced so well. And Dair performed his other two songs, playing piano, and electric and acoustic guitars.

The whole performance flew in, and then Dair and the dancers took their group bow to conclude the night.

Applause and cheers erupted from the audience, and although they were small in numbers, their enthusiasm was obvious.

Most people were on their feet, clapping, including Huntine and Cambeul.

There were a couple of moments when Dair locked eyes with Huntine, smiling at her, delighted with the show. Despite the energetic performance, Dair smiled brightly.

The photographer took group pictures of everyone involved in the show, and the line–up on stage included the show's tour director and costume designer.

As the last of the photographs were taken, Dair beckoned to Huntine to join him on stage.

She shook her head at him, reluctant to take any of the glory for the incredible performance.

'Go on,' Cambeul encouraged Huntine.

'I'm not part of the dancing,' she muttered to Cambeul.

'No, but your lyrics are part of the atmosphere created from the songs,' Cambeul countered. He ushered her up to the stage. Dair reached down, and with ease, lifted Huntine up to join him and the others for the last pictures of the night.

Dair stood upright with a strong, dancer's posture. Huntine and Shona stood on either side of him, along with the other dancers, and those involved in the performance and the show's tour.

At the end of the evening, everyone started to disperse, and Huntine decided to head home. Cambeul was engrossed in conversation with Shona. Dair was surrounded by the dancers and was discussing the show's plans with his tour director.

Although she hadn't expended a fraction of the energy the dancers had, Huntine felt the tiredness of a busy day of writing, followed by a highly–charged and entertaining evening, start to wash over her.

Catching Dair's attention for a moment from a distance, down in the audience area, she indicated that she was going home, but clearly showed that she'd loved the dance show.

For a moment, Dair looked like he was about to leap off the stage to talk to her, but he was swiftly wrapped in conversation about the dancing.

'Yes,' Dair confirmed to the other dancers. 'We'll have another rehearsal here tomorrow night at the dance studio.' It was booked, and there were numerous things they all wanted to practise and discuss having performed the full run through.

When Dair eventually looked around, Huntine had gone. Cambeul was still chatting with Shona and giving his opinion on the dance show, as a stage director. There were quite a few relevant things he mentioned, including his comments about the dance routine before the interval break.

'Invigorate the performance before the break with extra dance moves and dazzle,' Cambeul advised. 'I noticed you did this after the break, but always make the audience breathless with anticipation for more drama before the interval. It keeps the energy sparking, and the audience's chatter while they have a short break will be filled with extra enthusiasm. At least, in my experience of my work in the theatre. And your show is sheer spectacle and dancing drama.'

The colourful lights still shone on the stage where they were all standing. It created a bubble of vibrant chatter, and Dair was in the hub of it.

Huntine breathed in the brisk night air as she left the dance studio and walked to her car. The restaurants, cafes and bars were extra bright and busy, and her cream coat took on the different shades of the lights and glow from the windows.

She felt as if she'd stepped from one illuminated niche into another one. The first was fictional. The second was real. Her busy day of writing had led to her skipping dinner as she was running a bit late, and she'd wanted to arrive on time for the dance show.

During the interval break, she'd had a few sips of tea while discussing the performance with Cambeul. Then it was time for the second part of the show.

Now the night air refreshed her senses and she realised she could do with something to eat. Everywhere looked busy, so she drove home, leaving the extraordinary evening behind her, and Dair.

Arriving back, she changed out of her tea dress and dance shoes, and into comfy nightwear. Padding through to the kitchen, she started to make herself a light snack of cheese on toast, using thick–cut slices of farmhouse bread and Scottish cheddar.

Sitting in the living room by the cosy glow of a table lamp, she ate her cheesy toast and drank a mug of tea, while gazing out over the view of the city. Edinburgh looked particularly vibrant, hundreds of lights glittering, and the colours against the deep blue sky background reminded her of the stage setting from earlier. The atmosphere told a lively story of illuminations and entertainment.

She'd certainly been entertained that evening she thought, biting into a slice of her tasty toast. As she

188

was about to take a sip of her tea, a message popped up on her phone from Dair.

Sorry I didn't get a chance to talk to you before you left.

It's fine. The dance show was outstanding.

The routines were even better than I'd imagined they'd be when performed on stage.

All your hard work has paid off.

We're rehearsing at the dance studio tomorrow night. Will you be there? In the stage room, working on the play?

No, the following evening. I'll be snuggling in here to do my writing.

The disappointment hit him. *Well, good luck with your writing, and thanks for coming to the dance show tonight.*

It was a great night out.

The messages ended on a high note, but Huntine felt a sense of longing to talk to Dair, to phone and chat. Resisting the urge, she ate her cheesy toast, drank her tea, and instead of going to bed, she opened up her laptop and disappeared into her own fictional world of words.

Dair finally arrived home late at night, buzzing with the success of the evening. The photographer had previewed some of the pictures and video clips of the performance, and he could hardly wait to watch the edited version of the show in a couple of days time.

And the time was racing in. The dance tour began soon, with the opening night at a theatre in Edinburgh. Another second night in Edinburgh was followed by nights in other cities and towns, and Glasgow where he'd be dancing with Jessy, Huntine's grandmother. Hopefully Huntine would come to the Glasgow show if she was back home on the west coast.

Curious to see if their schedules intertwined, he checked the play's website on his laptop for specific dates. Comparing the dates, it was likely that she would be free to come to his dance show in Glasgow.

With this bolstering thought, Dair closed his laptop and made himself a mug of hot milk. Taking a sip, he took it through to the living room, then walked on to the dance floor. After the show, he'd changed out of his dance costume and into training gear.

Turning on some music, Dair started to dance, moving slowly to the rhythmic beat of the song. He danced his excess energy away, drank his milk and then went to bed, thinking of the show, the dance routines he'd practise the following night, and Huntine.

CHAPTER SIXTEEN

In the heart of the dance
You make me believe you are mine
In the heart of the waltz
We entwine
Under the spotlights just this time
Then you'll be gone
But I've loved our dance together
Sharing the stage with me
Then you'll be gone forever
A dance night memory...

Dair and the dancers practised one of the show's routines at the dance studio the following evening. They were all still buzzing with excitement from the previous night's performance — except Shona. Dair noticed that she was uncharacteristically subdued.

Usually, Shona would be bursting with chatter about the performance, but instead it was the others whose comments and laughter accompanied the rehearsal. Was she overtired, or overwrought, Dair wondered. And yet, she didn't look tired.

Without drawing attention to her quietude in front of the others, Dair whispered to her. 'Are you okay tonight?'

Eyes that looked like they were due to weep buckets, blinked out of her thoughts. 'Fine,' she lied.

Dair leaned closer. 'This is me you're lying to, Shona.'

A flick of the sad blue eyes acknowledged he was right, but she clearly had no intention of telling him her woes. At least, not while they were in the midst of a routine packed with lifts and complicated choreography.

Dair's nod assured her that she could change her mind later and tell him what was bothering her. They'd had their ups and downs over the years, but at the core, they'd always been friends. She knew she could rely on him. Shona hoped she could give him the same level of loyalty, and this was part of what was distressing her.

The surprise offer she'd had that morning was almost everything she currently wanted.

'From the top,' Dair announced, starting the music again.

Everyone took their positions as the intro played, and then burst into the choreography that cascaded from one style of dance to another. Ballroom, Latin, ceilidh — and those powerful lifts.

The music was upbeat, but changed beats, enabling Dair's choreography to accentuate the jumps and lifts.

Dair lifted Shona, again and again, and she performed with her usual high ability and on point timing.

But then it happened...

Shona turned the wrong way, and then she missed the set–up for a jump.

Dair stopped her as the others continued to dance. 'You've never missed this move before.' There was concern rather than censure in his comment.

Shona let go the breath she'd been holding in, along with the lie. 'I've got an opportunity to compete in the competition, but it's our opening night, so I won't do it.'

The weight of her predicament became apparent as she explained what had happened. Dair felt himself shoulder it too, hearing that the offer had come from his nearest rival, a top–class dancer and favourite to win the next big competition, and other titles that year.

'He heard me talk about wanting to take part in the dance competition when I phoned the Mullcairn radio show,' said Shona. 'He still had a partner then, but now they've had a big fall out and split up. She's found another partner, and he's asked me to partner with him.'

'You could win,' Dair assessed. 'I think you're a better dancer than his ex–partner.'

'We've a fair chance,' Shona agreed.

'Better than fair,' Dair emphasised. 'You could be the winning couple this year. Take home the trophy. A wonderful credit for your dancing career.'

'It's just rotten timing that the competition is being held on the same night as your show's opening in Edinburgh.' Shona shook her head. 'I won't let you down, Dair. I'd never do that. But I feel like I've been turned inside out.'

'You've always wanted to dance at this championship level,' he murmured in a confiding tone.

'I can't dance at the competition and be on stage for the show's opening night.' She sighed wearily. 'I'm not able to be in two places at the one time.'

'What if I could make it work for you, would you still do the rest of the tour?' he said, not knowing how he'd manage this.

'Yes, but it's not feasible, Dair,' she insisted, not wanting to get her hopes up.

'Leave it with me,' he said, and then held out his hand to her. 'Try the jump again.'

Shona took a steadying breath, and this time, she turned the right way and made the jump with her usual perfect timing.

The night had a chill wind that blew through Dair's hair as he walked out of the dance studio after the rehearsal evening and headed to his car.

The turmoil bubbled up inside him. He hadn't even zipped up his training top and the wind whipped it back to reveal the pale blue vest he was wearing. But he didn't feel the cold due to the upset burning in him.

He wasn't technically responsible for Shona's career. All dancers had to make tough choices about the work they accepted and rejected. Despite this, he felt emotionally responsible for Shona's career, especially when she could attain a credit that she'd have for the rest of her career. Shona could fight for herself, but he wouldn't be doing the right thing if he didn't try to find a mutually suitable way for her to compete and be part of the dance show.

Despondent, he dumped his bag in the car, and instead of getting in, he stood in the windy night, taking a deep breath of cold air to sharpen his senses, and phoned his tour director.

'Is there any chance we could change the date of the opening night?' Dair said, after explaining the predicament. He knew the answer, but he had to ask.

'I would if I could, but no, the theatre bookings can't be changed at this late date,' the tour director told him. 'Tickets are almost sold out, and it's a large venue, so there would be a lot of disappointed people if we messed with the opening night timing.'

'Thanks for a straightforward answer,' said Dair. 'I had to ask you.'

'I'm sorry, Dair.'

They bandied ideas around, all dead ends, except one that Dair threw into the ring.

'What if I could find a replacement for Shona, for one night, the opening night, would that work?' said Dair.

'Aye, that could work. Are you thinking of getting one of your other dancers to step into Shona's shoes, and find another backing dancer replacement?'

'No,' Dair sounded firm about this. 'I don't want to mess with the other dancers in the show. That would rattle everything from the top down and risk ruining the entire performance. It would put too much pressure on my dancers. That's not fair to them.'

'Someone you have in mind?'

Dair gazed at the lights of Edinburgh, feeling the breeze blow his hair back, clearing his thoughts, and gave the one–word solution to their problem.

'Huntine.'

'Do you think she'll do it? From what you've told me, she's never wanted to be in the dance spotlight.'

'I'm going to phone her. Wish me luck.'

Huntine typed the last paragraph of another chapter and relaxed back, easing the tension from her shoulders.

From the window of her flat, while working on her book, she'd watched the Edinburgh skyline emerge from the pink dawn to a bright morning, warm afternoon where it seemed that the remnants of spring were outshone by the early summer sun, and become a beautiful evening of glittering lights.

She was about to go through to the kitchen and make herself a cup of tea when Dair phoned her.

'Are you busy writing? Can I talk to you?'

'I've been writing all day, and just finished another chapter. What did you want to talk about?' she said, thinking he wanted to chat on the phone.

'Not on the phone.'

His tone made it sound important. 'Do you want me to drive over to your house?' she said.

'Could I drop by your flat? I won't stay long, but I'd prefer to discuss this with you tonight.'

'I'll put the kettle on.'

'I'm on my way.'

As she filled the kettle, she wondered what was so urgent and merited him visiting her that evening. She was still pondering this as she poured two mugs of tea and put them through in the living room, when Dair knocked on the door.

Huntine let him in and showed him through to the living room.

Dair stepped inside her cosy little flat, the hub of Huntine's writing world, and glanced around, taking in the homely feeling and the view from the window.

She sat down at the table near the window and Dair sat opposite her.

'Do you want something to eat?' she offered. 'Have you just come from the dance rehearsals?'

His stomach was knotted due to the current predicament. 'Tea's fine, thanks. And yes, I was at the dance studio. Shona was there, and that's what I want to talk to you about.' He summarised what had happened. 'After the rehearsals, I spoke to my tour director, and I suggested that I'd like to find someone to stand in for Shona for the opening night in Edinburgh.' He took a drink of his tea, gearing up to ask her. 'Would you like to take on the role, for one night?'

Huntine hadn't seen his offer coming and was taken aback. 'Dance with you, on stage for the opening night of your show?' she said, needing to clarify his offer.

'Yes. A one–off performance. Then Shona will continue the tour, hopefully after she's won the competition. My tour director also thinks that if she won the title, it would boost the tour, having a current champion as one of the principal dancers on the show. But it's more because I want Shona to have a chance to compete. If she wins, it'll be a credit she'll have to show what a wonderful dancer she is.'

'Is Shona okay about me stepping into her shoes?'

'She doesn't know. She's said that she'll forgo the contest and won't let me down. But I'm trying to find a way to make it work for everyone. I wanted to talk to you first, to see if you'd be willing to perform.'

Huntine took a steadying breath. 'You've certainly surprised me with this offer.'

'I'd pretty much need an answer soon. The tour starts in less than a week, and you'd need to be fitted for costumes.'

'I understand.' She took a sip of her tea. 'I'd like to help, but...I've never performed on stage in a theatre like this to a live audience.'

'I know, and my tour director is aware of this too. But you're such a tiger, Huntine.'

She laughed nervously. 'I wish.'

'You don't need to wish. I see the tiger in you. The wild side. The woman willing to challenge me, to take on tasks just because she likes a challenge. You didn't need to write my lyrics. You were already on a deadline for your novel. But you took on the task. And look where it led us. The extra interview, the Mullcairn show.' He looked lovingly at her. 'You've become a true friend. You inspire me to be a better man. I want to do right by Shona. And I'd love to dance the opening night performance on stage with you. Wouldn't that be a memory worth having? The night we stepped up to the challenge together.'

'Both a wee bit wild,' she said.

He opened his arms wide in a grand gesture. 'For one spectacular night.'

Huntine started to feel goosebumps at the thought of it. The challenge, the excitement, the experience of a lifetime, with Dair.

Dair looked at her. 'Say yes, Huntine.'

She felt her heart react to him, and then she glanced out the window at the glittering lights, picturing what it would be like to stand in the glittering spotlights of a magnificent stage, and dance.

Dair held his breath, waiting on her response. He'd already decided on the drive over that he wouldn't push her into doing it if she really didn't want to. But he hoped in his heart she would.

'Yes,' she said.

Dair couldn't contain his delight, and lifted her up as he cheered triumphantly.

Huntine started to laugh and squeal. 'You can put me down now.'

His strong arms wouldn't let her go, and he swung her around while he cheered and shouted. 'Yay! I hoped you would do it. I know you'll be great!'

'There will be a lot to organise,' she said as he finally put her down.

He agreed. 'Rehearsals. Costume fittings. More rehearsals. And a tight schedule. But you pick up the dance choreography fast. You've seen the full run through of the show. And you're a wonderful dancer. Those lifts you did with me, they're now part of the show's choreography.'

'I didn't think I'd be part of it,' she said, smiling at him.

'Surprise!'

Huntine laughed. 'I think I need another cup of tea.' She went through to the kitchen.

'I'll phone my tour director, and Shona, to tell them the news.'

While she made the tea, she heard him make the calls, and it seemed that they were both delighted with the plan, particularly Shona. Huntine imagined Shona would now phone Cambeul to tell him what she was going to be up to. The touch paper was about to be lit, creating a wildfire of gossip and anticipation in all their interconnected worlds.

Without asking him, Huntine buttered a treacle scone and a cheese scone, and took them through on a tray with the mugs of tea.

She blinked when she saw Dair standing at the window, finishing calling his tour director. He'd taken his outer top of to reveal the blue vest he was wearing. His broad–shouldered build was backlit by the glow of the lights from the window. Her heart fluttered, seeing him standing there, making her cosy wee flat even smaller, as this tall, handsome man made himself at home.

Dair put his phone away and eyed the scones and tea. 'A treacle scone?'

'Or cheese, take your pick.'

He picked the treacle scone. 'Did you anticipate I'd be coming here?'

'No. I'd bought a pack of four scones to keep me going today.'

He smiled hopefully. 'There's another treacle scone?' He'd hardly eaten anything all day due to being so busy.

She smiled tightly. 'Nope.'

'A spare cheese scone?'

'Out of luck there too.' She shrugged. 'It's been a long, busy day of writing.'

'Fired–up on scones,' he teased her.

'And Scotch broth. But I'm now ahead with my deadline,' she announced.

'We need to discuss how to work the dance rehearsals around your writing and the play.'

He lifted the treacle scone and took a bite. 'Tasty,' he mumbled.

Huntine bit into the cheese scone and nodded too.

For a few moments there was silence as they ate their scones. And then they started to laugh as neither of them could discuss anything while munching the scones.

Dair downed some of his tea, and began to formulate a plan. 'We'll talk to the costume designer tomorrow. And you can see if any of Shona's dresses fit you.'

'Shona is taller than me, and we've got different builds.' Huntine sounded concerned that the costumes wouldn't fit.

'The designer is an expert at making alterations to the clothes.'

'I'm sure she is, but that's not practical. Shona will be wearing them again for the next performance after mine.'

'That's true.' He was thinking of a solution when Huntine suggested something.

'The red dress Shona wore for one of the routines reminds me of the red dress I bought recently.'

'Can I see it?'

Huntine went through to the bedroom. Dair followed her, eager to help.

She opened the wardrobe. The red dress was hanging up with the others she'd bought recently. Lifting it out, she held it up for him to see. 'There's a fair bit of sparkle on it.'

'The costume designer could sparkle it up even more if needed.' Then he noticed the shimmering silver cocktail dress. 'What about this dress?'

'There weren't any dresses like this one in the show.'

'I know, but it's gorgeous and glitzy. I think you'd look great wearing it on stage under the lights.'

'Okay, so we've got two dresses that I could potentially wear.'

'Three.' Dair lifted out the hot pink design. 'Imagine this if it was sparkled up.'

Huntine nodded, picturing it would suit one of the dance routines.

He then peered into the wardrobe. 'Any other dresses hidden in there?'

'None with razzmatazz potential. Apart from the turquoise dress that isn't suitable for the show, they're all muted tones.'

'We'll chat to the costume designer tomorrow. I'll send her a message. But we've made a start on your costume conundrum.'

Huntine hung the dresses back in the wardrobe and closed the doors. As she turned around, Dair was standing there. She bumped into him and pressed her hands accidentally on his chest. Again, her fingers felt the lean, rippling strength of his body. Her heartbeat quickened feeling the wall of masculinity standing there in her bedroom.

Dair stepped back, pushing his hair away from his face, brushing his own wayward thoughts aside. Huntine could trust him not to overstep, even though he longed to take her in his arms, and not in a dance hold, in a lover's embrace.

He made light of the heavy situation and went back through to the living room and sat down to finish his tea and scone.

Huntine joined him and finished hers.

They discussed their plans.

'I'll make an announcement on my website that you'll be performing on the opening night,' he said. 'We'll tell everyone that Shona is competing, and for one night you're stepping in to dance with me.'

A rush of excitement charged through her at the thought of it. Dancing with Dare in the spotlight.

'Would you like to join me and dance the Highland Fling together? A special routine for a special night.'

'I'm tempted,' she said. 'I used to enjoy my Highland dancing.'

'Then dance it with me.'

Huntine smiled and nodded.

Dair finally stood up and put on his outer top. 'It's late, I'd better go and let you get some sleep.'

They'd agreed to meet in the morning at the costume designer's shop.

'I'll bring the three dresses with me,' Huntine said as she walked him out.

'Thanks again for stepping up and doing this. I know the dance show is the night after the opening of your play—'

'It's doable. The play is ready for the opening night. Cambeul has everything in hand. I'll attend the play's first night performance as planned.'

'And then dance with me the following night.' He admired her capability and energy.

'It seems like a fitting finale to our hectic time together.'

'Hectic and fun,' he said.

'Lots of fun.'

He almost forgot himself and went to lean down to kiss her goodnight, then awkwardly tried to hide this, stepped outside and walked over to his car. 'See you in the morning.'

Huntine smiled, nodded and waved him off.

She stood for a moment watching his car drive away, feeling an ache in her heart for Dair, and she wasn't sure how she'd feel when she went back to Glasgow.

Breathing in the night air, she gazed up at the vast sky, seeing a scattering of stars twinkle. Wondering what it would be like to dance on stage under the spotlights, her stomach knotted anxiously, and then released when she told herself she wanted this memory. The night she performed to a live audience, dancing with Dair.

CHAPTER SEVENTEEN

Waltz into my world again
Partner with me once more
We were always meant to be
Romancing on the dance floor
I hold you close as we dance
No one feels the way you do
Waltz into my life again
For me, it's always been you...

Dair thought he wouldn't sleep that night, but he was so tired he fell asleep without even realising, and woke refreshed the next morning.

He checked the time, and then jumped in the shower and got ready to meet Huntine for the costume fittings.

Parking fairly near the premises, he walked along to the costume shop and saw Huntine walking towards the premises from the opposite direction. She was smartly dressed in her grey tones. But her muted ensemble of trousers, a blouse and jacket were due to be elevated into a bright, sparkly dance costume bubble.

In the distance, Huntine saw the tall figure wearing his casual dancewear training gear, walking towards her. There was no mistaking his rhythmic gait, the way he walked showed the dancer in him. Her heartbeat quickened as he saw her and stepped up his pace.

He strode towards her, smiling. 'Shall we go in?' He gestured to the shop's creative niche, seeing that the lights were on inside the premises.

Huntine nodded, and held up the bag of dresses she'd brought with her. 'I came armed and ready to sparkle.'

Whatever she'd pictured the costume designer's shop would look like, this wasn't it. In a brilliant, dazzling, costume emporium way.

The bright spotlights shone on the rails of fantastic dance clothes, all vintage or pre–loved, worn for shows in the recent past or long ago. The premises was light and airy, while brimming with rich fabrics and ornate embellished dresses, tops, skirts, shirts and jackets.

Bundles of newly arrived dancewear were perched on the long counter that stretched over to the changing rooms. The costume designer and her assistants were already hard at work, cutting paper patterns, snipping lengths of fringing from the edges of dresses, and sewing on strips of sequins. Their early start was usual, and not due to Dair and Huntine's scheduled meeting.

Two mannequins wore calico toiles, being fashioned by the designer into the basis of garments using pre–loved costumes and fabric, ready to have strips of sequins and beading sewn on. The mock–ups of the costumes were vintage–modern styles.

The costume designer smiled, happy to welcome in Dair and Huntine.

'I see you have a bag there,' the costume designer observed. 'What did you bring with you?'

Huntine showed her the three dresses.

The costume designer held up the red dress and nodded her approval. 'Nice. This has tons of potential. Is it a neat fit on you?'

'It is,' Huntine confirmed.

'Could you pop into the changing room and put it on?'

Huntine smiled and disappeared behind the curtained changing room, and then stepped out again wearing the red dress, along with a pair of her champagne ballroom dance shoes. She'd pinned her hair up in a ballet bun secured with a butterfly clasp so that the shoulders and neckline could be seen.

The costume designer stood back and assessed the dress. 'In real life, perfect, just the right amount of subtle sparkle and frou–frou. For stage wear, it needs more dazzle.' She reached for two rolls of sequins, one red, one gold, and began to pin pieces on from just below the waistline to the hem, as if the sparkle was cascading down the dress. 'Take a look in the mirror.'

Huntine stepped in front of the full–length mirror beside the counter and turned back and forth, causing the sequins to glitter like sparks in a fire.

'This looks gorgeous,' Huntine enthused.

'It does,' Dair agreed. 'It's for a tango type of routine, quite dramatic.'

'I'll have the sequins stitched on,' the costume designer told them. 'And I'd wear gold ballroom dance shoes with this dress.'

Huntine noted the recommendation. 'I have a pair of those.'

Next up was the silver cocktail dress. The fabric shimmered like liquid silver under the lights. The costume designer loved it. 'This dress doesn't need any work, and wear silver ballroom shoes with it. But...I have a silver boa that would be an ideal accessory, if it fits with the routine.'

Huntine draped the tinsel–like silver boa around her neck, and they agreed it would be used to accessorise the dress.

The pink dress was then assessed and scheduled to be given a scattering of pink sequins to it.

'Are you wearing any of Shona's dresses?' said the costume designer.

'Maybe one or two, depending on the fit,' Huntine explained, while looking at the numerous beautiful dresses on the rails.

'It's a one–night performance, and then Shona will be back the following night, so her costumes can't be altered,' said Dair.

The costume designer noticed Huntine looking at a rail of dresses. 'These arrived recently.' She picked out a dazzling purple dress that was split to the thigh and draped with chiffon. 'You'd suit this. Try it on.'

Huntine glanced at Dair, and he nodded. 'We'll need at least four extra dresses for you to wear at the show, apart from the red, silver and pink.'

While Huntine was getting changed, she heard Dair and the costume designer chatting about other dresses in stock.

'This is stunning.' Dair held up a dancewear, cocktail–style dress in shades of aqua blues, fading from the palest to the deepest tones around the hemline. The fabric was shot through with metallic blue thread, and a sequin effect emphasised the bodice and decorated the shoestring straps.

'It's vintage, but in lovely condition.' The costume designer read the note attached. 'The dress was worn for a tour years ago and then put into storage. It's a one–off, so if you're interested, it'll be a real bargain. And...I've got another dress that I've had for a while. It's so standout that it hasn't fitted in with any costume designs for shows. And it's a very neat style.' She handed it and the aqua dress through the curtain to Huntine. 'Try these on too.'

Huntine hung them up in the changing room and then emerged wearing the dazzling purple dress.

Dair and the costume designer gave it the thumbs up.

'I'll put a couple of darts in the waistline to make it a neater fit for you,' the costume designer told Huntine.

'The purple tones will match the other dancers' outfits in some of the routines,' said Dair.

Huntine then put the aqua dress on. Minor tucks were required to make it fit. The dazzling standout dress fitted ideally, but the straps needed more sequins.

These dresses were then added to a rail, and marked to be adjusted or embellished for Huntine.

'We're both performing a Highland Fling,' Dair confided. 'Is there anything in your Scottish costume rail that would suit Huntine?'

The costume designer brightened. 'I have a few Highland ensembles.' She picked one up. 'This should fit.' She handed the white blouse, kilt and waistcoat into the changing room where Huntine was getting dressed.

Huntine felt at home wearing the Highland outfit. The blouse had elbow–length sleeves, the tartan kilt was just above knee–length, and the velvet waistcoat completed the outfit.

'This feels great,' said Huntine. 'I could certainly dance in this, wearing fine tartan, knee–length socks and ghillie shoes.'

The costume designer didn't have the socks or shoes, but suggested a shop that sold these new. And then she added a suggestion. 'Would you like me to add a bit of sparkle to your kilt outfit?'

Huntine glanced at Dair and they both nodded.

The kilt outfit was then hung beside the other dresses on the rail.

'Everything will be ready in a couple of days,' the costume designer assured them. 'I know you need the dresses in a hurry.'

Happy that the costumes were being sorted out, Dair and Huntine then left, and bought the fine, knee–length tartan socks and ghillie shoes.

Huntine popped them in her bag.

'Apart from trying on a couple of Shona's dresses, I think your costumes are sorted,' said Dair. He'd paid for storage of the show's costumes at the dance studio.

Dair had dance rehearsals at the studio later, and Huntine had rehearsals for the play.

'Maybe you could try on the costumes after the play's rehearsal this evening,' Dair suggested.

'Yes, I'd like to see if they fit.'

'What are you doing now?' he said, glancing around, expecting her to head to her car and drive off home.

'Nothing planned.' Her tone left her open to suggestions.

'Do you want to come home with me? We could practise the choreography in the living room for a few hours, and then head to the dance studio together tonight. After you've tried the costumes on, and the others have gone, we could practise a few routines.'

'Dancing for hours now, and then more dancing in the evening.' She pretended to ponder this hectic schedule. 'I'm up for it if you are.'

'We can take my car,' he suggested.

'No, I'll follow you in mine. I have stuff in it that I threw together this morning, in case I needed it.'

'What type of stuff?'

'Dance emergency stuff. Whenever I'm around you, I'm either doing a foxtrot, quickstep, waltzing, being thrown about the dance floor or whirling around in a ceilidh routine.'

'I'm glad you came prepared. Those are exactly the things I had in mind,' he teased her.

She smiled, unsure how close to the mark her comment was.

He headed towards his car and cast a comment back to her. 'And a Highland Fling.'

Huntine walked away. 'No ballet?'

She heard him laugh, and then headed to her car to follow him back to his house.

When they arrived at Dair's house he helped her in with the bags of stuff she'd brought with her.

Huntine carried her laptop and the new ghillie brogues and socks he'd bought for her. He'd insisted on paying for everything, assuring her he could afford it without reminding her that he was wealthy.

They went into the living room and he gestured to a room that was just off it. 'You can take your clothes off in there.'

The look Huntine gave him made him rephrase his comment. 'If you want to get changed into whatever you've brought with you.'

'I'll do that,' she said, and went through and closed the door.

He opened the patio doors, letting the fresh air and sunlight pour in. Then he ran upstairs, took off his casual jacket to reveal a black vest that he was wearing with his black training trousers, put on his dance shoes and ran back downstairs.

Huntine was still getting changed, so he made them a quick cup of tea and brought the two mugs through in time for her to emerge wearing an elegant dancewear outfit consisting of slim–fitting, high–waist black leggings and a black, sleeveless fitness top worn with the ghillie brogues.

They looked at each other and smiled, seeing how well they unintentionally matched.

'We look like we're dressed in dance stealth mode,' she remarked.

He laughed and handed her a mug of tea.

She took a few sips as he suggested what they'd practise.

'I've adapted the Highland Fling for the stage performance,' he explained. 'There are traditional Scottish dance steps in it, but mixed with modern stage choreography.'

'I noticed this during the filming of the run through.' She'd danced the Highland Fling for years and recognised the changes he'd made.

He put his mug down, and so did Huntine.

'Do you want to try it? I'll run through the steps first, and then put some music on.'

Huntine was up for this.

After he showed her the sequence of the routine, they stood side by side on the dance floor as the Scottish theme music began.

They danced various steps, including toe–and–heel steps, back–stepping, crossovers, and other steps, hands on their waists, then one arm raised, sometimes two, keeping in time to the music. Then this part merged with the modern stage moves.

Dair let the music continue while they repeated the dance routine. Finally, he stopped and smiled at her. 'Wonderful.'

'I enjoyed that,' she admitted.

'Shall we run through another couple of numbers?' he said, suggesting the opening routine where he'd be singing and playing while she performed with the other dancers before he joined in.

Dair took on the role of one of the other dancers to allow Huntine to practise the routine.

'Your choreography makes sense to me,' she said. 'There are no awkward moves, especially when the

213

dance styles merge. It whips up a lot of emotion and energy.'

'I'm pleased you understand what I've tried to create with the choreography.'

They continued to dance for the next hour, and had only just stopped for a short break when Huntine's grandmother phoned — Dair.

'Hello, Jessy,' Dair said, taking the face–to–face call, and seeing the surprised look on Huntine's face that her grandmother was phoning him.

'I wanted to thank you for the tickets for the opening show in Edinburgh,' said Jessy. 'And the hotel booking. That was very generous of you.'

Jock leaned over his wife's shoulder, smiling, and joined in the conversation, unaware that Huntine was there.

'We're looking forward to staying in the lovely hotel,' said Jock.

'I'm glad you'll both be coming along to the show,' Dair told them.

'We wouldn't miss Huntine's performance with you on the opening night,' Jessy said, sounding excited. 'We're going to phone her and—'

'Huntine's here, rehearsing the dance routines with me.' Dair turned the phone around to show them their granddaughter.

Her grandparents' faces lit up and they waved to her.

'We're delighted that you're stepping in for Shona,' said her grandmother. 'But you'll give a fine performance, Huntine. And we'll be in the audience to cheer you on.'

'I hope you don't mind sitting next to Mullcairn and his friend, Etta,' Dair told them.

'Mullcairn!' Jessy squealed. 'I listen to his radio show all the time. Oh, this night just gets more exciting by the moment.'

Dair gave Jock a knowing look. Jock winked back at him, unseen by Jessy, but Huntine noticed. She frowned at Dair, but he didn't address the exchange, and continued to chat lightly.

'Well, it was handy that Huntine was there with you,' said Jessy. 'We'll let the two of you get on with your dance practise.' Waving and smiling, Jessy and Jock were gone.

Huntine hadn't uttered a word to her grandparents, but felt like she'd been part of the conversation. But Dair was up to skulduggery, and she wanted to know what it was.

'Jock knows, but you can't tell Jessy. It'll spoil the surprise,' said Dair.

'What do you mean?'

'You know that I've arranged tickets for your grandparents to come along to one of the shows in Glasgow, and that I've invited Jessy to come up on stage and dance with me.'

'Yes, she's delighted. She's even started thinking what dress she'll wear when she joins you on stage.'

'Well, I'm doubling up on the dance invitation for Jessy,' he revealed. 'Jock will escort her up on to the stage at the Edinburgh show, along with a handful of others from the audience during the break.'

'Gran gets to dance with you twice! In Glasgow and Edinburgh!' Huntine exclaimed, knowing how much her grandmother would love this.

'Jock's dancing too. A waltz.'

Huntine smiled. 'Waltzing with Jessy on stage!'

'Not with Jessy. With you.'

She blinked. 'My grandfather's going to waltz with me on stage on the opening night?' She needed to clarify this before cheering.

'Yes, while I'm waltzing with Jessy.'

A surge of emotion rose up inside her. 'You've organised this?'

Dair nodded. 'With Jock being in on the sneaky plans. We want to surprise Jessy.'

'Surprise my grandmother! You've totally surprised me.'

'A bonus,' Dair said with a grin.

'I couldn't let this special night go by without some sort of personal celebration,' he explained. 'Your grandparents are proud of your dancing. But this is the first time you'll perform on stage. Probably the last too. Your parents can't come because they're down south on business. But, I've hired the photographer and videographer to film the performance. I want to look back on it too. We'll all get a copy to watch you dancing at the show. Jock says Jessy will treasure it.'

Huntine blinked back the happy tears that were welling up. 'Thank you, Dair. That's so kind and thoughtful. I know my grandparents will both treasure the video, and the trip to Edinburgh. It's the perfect gift.'

Wiping away a stray tear, she stepped close to Dair, and on tip–toe gave him a soft kiss on the cheek.

This gesture said it all.

Dair felt the emotion well up inside him too. Her first kiss was from the heart, and he sensed it touch his heart deeply. In the depths of the night, when he let his thoughts drift to romance with Huntine, he'd pictured their first kiss, if it ever happened, would be one of passion and desire. The sweetness of this first kiss was somehow more memorable.

'Shall we try another routine?' he suggested, clearing his throat.

'Yes, what do you suggest?'

'The cheeky cha–cha–cha number that includes a sassy salsa.' He went over and put on suitably upbeat music with the right rhythm for these dances.

Huntine faced Dair, ready to cha–cha, recalling seeing the routine. Shona had put a lot of energy into it.

The upbeat song lifted the mood, and soon they were dancing around the floor.

'Give it some more...' Dair frowned, trying to find the right word.

'Vibrancy?'

Dair shook his head. 'Va–va–voom!'

Huntine laughed, and hit the energy button on the routine.

They danced until it was time for a light dinner before heading to the dance studio. In the kitchen, they rustled up lentil soup with thick slices of bread, and ate it while planning the evening ahead. Huntine would rehearse the play with Cambeul. Dair would rehearse with the dancers, minus Shona. She was practising with her new partner for the competition.

When it was time to go, Huntine put her coat on over her dancewear, and Dair helped her take her bags and laptop out to her car.

They drove in tandem to the studio, and went their separate ways in the corridor.

Huntine sat down beside Cambeul in the stage room as the actors rehearsed parts of the play's third act.

She took her coat off and put it over the back of her chair, revealing her dancewear.

Cambeul didn't disguise his reaction. 'You're dressed like a dancer, like Shona!' he whispered in a surprised hiss.

'I've been rehearsing the dances with Dair all day, after visiting the costume designer.' She kept her voice down.

'You suit your hair in a ponytail like that, very swishy.'

'How are things with you and Shona?'

'She's steeped in dance rehearsals for the competition, so she says she'll just have to phone me more often until after the contest.' Cambeul made a fist. 'I'm inwardly cheering for her.'

Huntine smiled at him. 'I wish Shona all the luck.'

When the stage play rehearsal finished, Huntine went along to the dance room. Music filtered out, and she was now so familiar with the songs that she knew what dance they were practising.

Opening the door, she stepped in and sat down without causing a ripple.

Dair and the dancers were performing a routine where they intertwined classic ballroom waltzing with a foxtrot.

When they finished, Dair turned the music off, and the dancers came over and hugged Huntine, wrapping her in welcoming smiles, answering her unspoken concerns about what they thought about her stepping in for Shona.

Dair joined them, and encouraged Huntine to put her dancing shoes on and run through the routine with them before they finished their rehearsals.

Huntine had brought her dance shoes in her bag, currently armed at all times with shoes she could wear if she needed to practise the choreography.

Dair put the music on, and stood beside Huntine at the front of the small ensemble, facing the mirror.

Seeing herself standing there, dressed in her dancewear, reflected the life she could have had. Nothing made her want to rewind and choose dancing over her writing career, but this was a side pocket in time where she could venture down the dancing route as part of a spectacular show. Her years of dance training, finally coming to the fore when she needed it.

Huntine danced well. The dancers had seen the video clips on Dair's website of her dancing with him. But here, she was exposed in the full light of the rehearsal room. This was the first time they'd seen Huntine dance live, and it was clear that she was a skilled and elegant dancer.

When the rehearsals finished and the dancers headed out, chatting happily, Dair took Huntine along to the small room where the show's costumes were stored. He took a key from his pocket, unlocked the door and switched the light on as they stepped inside.

The costumes were hanging on rails, and the fabrics and sequins glittered under the light.

'Shona's costumes are over here on this rail.' Dair showed her the selection hanging up. It included the purple dress she'd worn when ruffling Cambeul's hair, and the finale's fairytale pink ballgown.

'I'll step outside into the corridor while you try the dresses on,' he said, leaving her to choose any that fitted.

The first dress she put on was the purple one as it looked like a wrap style, easy to put on for a quick costume change, and the chiffon skirt was in wispy points making the length of the hemline suitable for her.

She opened the door. 'What do you think of this dress?' She gave him a twirl.

'Oh, yes, that's lovely,' he confirmed.

'Be back with the next one in a minute.' Huntine closed the door and put on a blue confection that had a dreamlike quality, and again, the handkerchief points of the chiffon that was scattered with glitter, worked length–wise and on the short sleeves.

Huntine opened the door again and fluffed the chiffon fabric on the shirt. 'This is a dream to wear.'

'It's ideal,' he agreed.

'This would give me two dresses that would make me match the other dancers,' Huntine reasoned. 'If I wear the same outfits as them for a couple of the routines, it'll help me look part of the show. Then when I wear the other dresses, my costumes will seem less of an eclectic mix.'

Dair nodded. 'This would work. The costumes and lighting are designed to replace any need for sets and scenery,' he explained. 'The dancing, music, lighting and costumes create the atmosphere on stage. It allows us to go from one theatre to the next without any huge sets needing to be transported for the one or two–night performances.'

Huntine understood. 'The play has core sets, and we're relying on lighting effects too. But we're performing for a week or more at each theatre, so we've more time to organise sets.'

The pink ballgown was the next dress Huntine tried on.

'This feels wonderful,' Huntine said to Dair, showing him the beautiful ballgown. The dress comprised of a rose pink bodice flowing into a full skirt in shades of pink that faded to the palest pink towards the hemline glistening with sparkles.

'You look like you've stepped out of a fairytale.' Then he gestured to a rail where his costumes were hanging up. 'I'm wearing this when I'm waltzing with you.' It was a classic black evening suit with a white shirt and turquoise blue bow tie that was a fair match for his eyes.

Huntine pictured him wearing this for the romantic dance finale.

'There's a stage kiss at the end of the dance,' he told her. 'I'm sure you know what this is.'

'An almost kiss. Angled so the audience thinks we've truly kissed, but we stop a breath apart.'

Dair's heart thundered thinking about kissing Huntine. How he longed to take her in his arms right now and kiss the breath from her.

'That's right,' he replied calmly. 'We'll practise it when we rehearse the waltz choreography that has lifts and showpiece moves included.'

'Yes, we wouldn't want to make a mistake and actually kiss on stage in front of the whole audience.'

'Certainly not.' He heard himself say this, but his heart didn't entirely go along with it. Shaking himself out of thoughts of romancing Huntine, he tried to sound chirpy. 'Well, that's the costumes organised. We'll pick up the dresses from the costume designer when they're ready. Apart from that, I think you're ready for the ball, Cinderella.'

'And then change back to being the wordsmith after the show ends.' She sounded wistful. No romantic fairytale ending for her. But she'd reconciled herself to this, and was already realising that the dancing and lyrics bubble she was in there in Edinburgh was due to be over in less than a week. Glasgow was beckoning, and now she was nearer to the end of her story in Edinburgh than the beginning.

'You look sad.'

Sometimes his blunt observations took her breath away, and she replied with equal openness. 'I was just thinking that I'll be heading back to Glasgow in a few days.'

He knew this, but hearing her state it hit him so hard that he was sure she sensed how he felt.

'We've had fun.' He fought to sound upbeat.

'A wild time.' She fought alongside him.

'It's not over yet,' he reminded her.

'No, I've the play's opening night on the evening before the dance show.'

'I'm sure the play will be a success,' he said.

'It's turned out really well. The actors, Cambeul's direction, the stage lighting to create the mood of the past. I'm more confident about the play than I am about my performance for the dance show.'

'You should be confident about both. And I'm doubly confident that you'll dance beautifully on stage.'

Huntine smiled. 'You sound like my personal cheerleader.'

Dair punched the air playfully. 'Ra! Ra! Ra!'

Laughing, Dair stood outside while Huntine changed out of the pink ballgown and into her own clothes.

She stepped out into the corridor and flicked the storeroom light off. Dair locked the door, and they walked down the corridor and outside into the night.

The air was mild, and they walked by the restaurants and eateries towards their cars.

'What's your schedule for tomorrow?' he said as they walked along together.

'Dance rehearsals in the morning, afternoon and night,' she replied, half joking.'

'At my house?'

'I don't think there's much room to tango or foxtrot in my wee flat.'

'I could manage to lift you up and twirl you around. You'd enjoy the view from your window from a whole new angle.'

'Tempting as that offer is, I'm going to go with my first option — your house.'

'Breakfast at nine?'

By now they'd reached their cars.

'I'll bring something tasty,' she said getting into her car.

'My plan worked perfectly.' He waved as she drove off and called to her. 'Treacle scones would be nice!'

He was sure he heard her laughing through the open window.

Dair ran and got into his car to follow her, and they again drove in tandem until the turnoffs took them in separate routes home.

Huntine got ready for bed as soon as she arrived home. Wise enough to know that sitting up late writing wouldn't bode well when she had such a hectic dance schedule the next day.

Lying in bed, she tugged the quilt up, and gazed out the window, rewinding wearing the fairytale ballgown and thinking about practising the stage kiss.

She could still remember the touch of Dair's lips as they'd accidentally brushed against each other days ago. Now, she had to pretend to kiss Dair.

But that was the story of her life, lived in a world of wonderful make believe where happy ever afters were assured. No fairytale real life ending for her, she told herself as she fell sound asleep.

Huntine woke up early, feeling refreshed, and managed to get an hour's writing done before popping to the grocery shop for treacle scones and other tasty breakfast treats.

Dair was dancing in the kitchen, wearing a vest, training trousers and dance shoes, when she arrived at the back door and let herself into the kitchen.

'Morning!' She put the two bags of groceries down.

The smile he gave her warmed her heart.

She took her coat off to reveal she was wearing black leggings, a pink top and her training shoes. And she'd brought other dance shoes, including her ghillie brogues, and her laptop with her.

'What are we indulging in today?' He peered into the grocery bags.

'Sort of a repeat of what we had before. I thought, go with what worked. I added tins of broth and leek and potato soup in case we needed an easy lunch. And a large, fresh crusty loaf as well as a sliced one. All angles covered on the bread front, including Scottish breakfast rolls.'

'A feast indeed.' Dair fired up the grill to cook the slices of Lorne sausage like they'd had before, while Huntine prepared the slices of bread and set the tea and plates up.

They sat down at the kitchen table to enjoy breakfast, and spoke about the dance routines, what they'd tackle first that day.

After breakfast, they went through to the living room. As Dair opened the patio doors to let the fresh morning air in, a call came through for Huntine from Cambeul.

'The theatre producer phoned me about the Christmas play. He's had excellent feedback about the dancing we're adding to the show.'

'That's great,' said Huntine.

'Yes, but now he wants the role of the leading lady dancer emphasised more. Instead of helping him find someone who can act and has dancing skills, he wants a dancer who can act.' It wasn't the lead acting role, but it was the principal dancer's role.

Dair sat on the piano stool and could hear the conversation.

'Okay,' she agreed. 'But I don't have anyone in mind.'

'I do,' said Cambeul.

'Who?'

'Shona. She started out in drama school, training in acting and in dance. She'd wanted to work in musical theatre. But her skill in dancing led her to focus on dance.'

'Shona can act?' Huntine sounded surprised.

'Oh, yes, and we know she's an excellent dancer,' Cambeul confirmed.

'I'm with Dair. Hang on a minute.' Huntine put the phone on speaker and looked over at Dair. 'Did you know that Shona can act?'

'Yes, Shona intended working in musical theatre, but her dancing took precedence,' said Dair.

Huntine looked hopeful. 'Shona could fit the character I've written.'

'I'll phone Shona and tell her,' said Cambeul.

226

'No!' Dair called out. 'Don't tell Shona until after the dance competition. You could disrupt her concentration, jeopardise her winning.'

'You're right,' Cambeul agreed. 'I'll keep my lips buttoned. I'll tell her after the competition. Either way, if she wins the title or not.'

Agreeing on their plan, they finished the call on a hopeful note.

Huntine and Dair did their warm–up exercises. He opted for a lot of floor stretches, working his powerful muscles.

She used the back of one of the chairs to practise her ballet barre routine that kept her flexible and strong, and improved her posture. Holding lightly to the chair, she began with plié moves, starting in first position, extending her hand out gracefully to the side, she performed a demi–plié, a half bend, followed by a grand plié, a full bend.

He was quietly impressed with her ballet barre routine, and it was clear that she practised this on a regular basis.

Then they got ready to rehearse, having decided they'd practise a ceilidh routine that included modern stage. And then moved on to the ballroom numbers.

After quickstepping and waltzing around going over the short routine a few times, they stopped for a tea break.

Huntine sat on the piano stool reading the music sheet that was propped up on the piano stand, while Dair made the tea and brought it through.

'Is this your new song? The one from the past that you never finished?' She recognised the brief lyrics that still had gaps for the missing words.

Dair nodded. 'I've been taking your advice, trying to write the lyrics myself from how I feel about everything. I've added a few lines for a verse. I'm playing most of it on piano, but the opening riff and other parts on electric guitar.'

'I'd love to hear the guitar sections.'

His sensual lips curved into a smile, and he picked up his electric guitar from the stand where it was plugged in, slung the strap over his shoulders, and began to play.

There was something so sexy about seeing him play electric guitar, as if she had a glimpse into a deeper, sensual side of him. Or perhaps it was just that she found him extra gorgeous when he was playing guitar while wearing his dance training gear. The muscles in his arms and shoulders were a definite distraction. Part of her wished she hadn't encouraged him. Part of her was delighted she had.

Dair played but didn't sing the lyrics. The sound from the guitar resonated through the living room and through Huntine. The notes sent waves of excitement through her and her heartbeat quickened.

It quickened even more when Dair walked over to her, took the guitar off and hung the strap over her shoulders.

'I can't play,' she said, giggling, and yet not resisting what it felt like to hold the beautiful guitar. It was heavier than she'd imagined, but the strap kept it steady, and the design of it was so well–balanced that it felt right.

Towering above her, and so close she could see the flecks of deeper blue in those turquoise eyes of his, Dair adjusted the strap to suit her. Then he placed her hands on the frets, and gave her a small plectrum so she could strum and pluck the strings.

Her laughter, and willingness to have a go, warmed his heart. He'd never met anyone like Huntine Grey. He doubted he ever would again.

Dair stepped behind her, leaning over. With his arms around her, his hands guided hers, showing her how to play a chord.

'It sounds like I'm twanging it all wrong,' she said, smiling.

He laughed and adjusted her hands, and at the touch of his strong but elegant fingers, her heart went wild, and she had to force herself to calm down. But most women in her situation would find Dair attractive, she told herself, especially as he was standing so close, and she could feel his muscles pressed against her.

This time, she played it a lot better, though she knew her talents were not in playing the guitar.

'Is this a ruse to teach me to play guitar, so that I can accompany you when you're playing piano on stage?' she joked. 'Because if it is, let me tell you, I can see through all your sneaky schemes.'

Dair stepped back and laughed. 'Thwarted again,' he said, joining in the joke, and helped take the guitar off her and placed it back on the stand.

Huntine pretended to check the time. 'And that was a sleekit move to get a longer break from the dance practise.'

Dair played along. 'There's no fooling you.'

They started rehearsing again, but she could still feel the excitement resonating in her heart. And he fought not to let himself care for her so much that his heart would be torn to pieces when she went home to Glasgow soon.

'We should practise the waltz,' he said after they'd finished another routine. 'It's part of the show's finale.'

'When I wear the pink ballgown?'

'The bit where we do the stage kiss.'

A nervous fluttering erupted inside her. 'Yes, we don't want to get that wrong.'

He gazed down at her. 'Do you want to try it before we dance the waltz?'

'Okay.' Her reply was higher–pitched than she'd intended, surely giving away her nervousness.

Dair stepped close, facing her, still gazing down. 'Look up at me, then turn your head to the left slightly, while I turn mine to the right. Keep your back to the audience, so that the angle of our kiss seems right to them, while we actually don't lock lips.'

'I turn my head to the right—'

'No, you turn to the left,' he cut–in.

He showed her how the move worked, causing all sorts of fireworks to ignite inside her.

'Got it,' she said, unsure that she had it nailed. There were too many emotions washing over her. Then she took charge of her feelings, taking a deep breath, and telling herself to get it right. While turning left. Right?

'Are you okay, Huntine?'

'Yes,' she lied. 'I think I'm still buzzing from the electric guitar, and overloaded with all the dance routines.'

'We can take a break,' he offered, his eyes gazing at her with genuine kindness. 'I'll make you a cuppa.'

'No, let's do this,' she insisted. How hard could it be pretending to kiss Dair?

Harder than she imagined, as she missed the first cue. 'That was silly of me.'

'Try again, slowly.'

She took a deep breath. How could it be that it was easier to do complicated lifts and fast–moving modern stage choreography than pretend to kiss Dair? She scolded herself for the umpteenth time. Get your act together, she told herself firmly.

'Okay, I'm ready,' she said.

This time, she got it right. But Dair got it wrong, and accidentally kissed her, sending them both into an embarrassing moment.

'Sorry, I...sorry,' he mumbled an apology while feeling his heart pounding with the passion her lips ignited in him.

'It's fine. I think we should move on to the waltz. I'll change my shoes.' Huntine hurried over to where her ballroom dance shoes were, took off her brogues, and put them on.

They waltzed around the floor, practising the routine.

'The storyline for this part of the show is that the characters finally fall in love. A romantic ending,' he said.

'The song is beautiful,' she said. A popular classic. Perfect for waltzing around the stage in a ballgown.

'Everyone is on stage for the last part of the finale sequence.'

'You've created a wonderful show,' she said.

Dair smiled and then suggested they stop for lunch.

They went through to the kitchen.

'Broth or leek and potato?' he said. There were two tins of each.

'Leek and potato.'

He opened two tins of the leek and potato soup and heated them up while Huntine cut thick slices of bread to go with it.

After lunch, they rehearsed until the amber glow of the late afternoon sun faded into twilight.

'I think we've rehearsed enough,' said Dair.

'Yes, but now I feel more confident about performing on stage.'

They agreed to practise more in the coming days, at his house, and at the dance studio with the other dancers. And that's what they did. They also had a few dress rehearsals. The costume designer had done a wonderful job of Huntine's dresses.

On the evening before the opening night of Huntine's play, she had her final rehearsal with Dair and the dancers at the studio.

They had a rehearsal scheduled at the theatre where the dance show would have it's opening night.

Huntine wouldn't be there for the final rehearsal. She had to give her full attention to the play. Cambeul had taken up a lot of the strain while she'd split her time between the play and the dancing. Now the play took priority, as agreed with Dair.

He wouldn't be able to attend the play's opening night as he'd be working on the dance show's final rehearsal at the theatre. But he planned to attend one of the performances another night.

On the play's opening night, Huntine arrived with Cambeul at the theatre. It was aglow with lights and posters advertising the play. The tickets had sold out, and the wordsmith and stage director walked in alongside those turning up to watch the play. Two figures going unnoticed in the buzz of activity as everyone went inside and sat ready for the curtain going up.

Cambeul and Huntine went backstage to check that everyone was set for the performance. Then they took their seats in the audience.

Cambeul had brought a packet of chocolate buttons with him. As the lights dimmed for the start of the play, he offered her some.

'Thanks, Cambeul,' she whispered. She took a few, and so did he.

It had become their little celebratory routine over the time they'd worked together on the plays, sharing a packet of chocolate buttons and settling down to watch the opening night.

It was just Huntine and Cambeul, and a full theatre audience eager to see the play. Huntine's grandparents were going to see the play when it showed in Glasgow.

As the lights dimmed and the curtain rose, the play began...

At the end of the performance, Huntine and Cambeul joined the cast on stage as the audience applauded. From the audience's reaction, the play was a success.

Huntine celebrated with Cambeul and the cast backstage, before finally heading home.

It was the start of the play's tour, but she was closer to the end of her time in Edinburgh. Looking out the window of her flat when she got home that night, she realised how she only had the dance show performance the following night, and then she'd be packing her bags and heading back to Glasgow.

The plan with Cambeul was, as usual, she'd go home to Glasgow, and write the next play, while working on her novels. This plan had worked well for them so far. This year, there was the increased demand for her plays, one for the autumn and the Christmas play, but this was what she wanted, and Cambeul would be directing. She'd already written the Christmas play, and part of the autumn one, so it was doable.

Recently, despite the hectic dance rehearsals with Dair, she'd managed to squeeze in pockets of writing. She was still ahead of schedule for her deadline. Work was fine. Her feelings for Dair were the issue. She'd kept that guard up strong, even though he'd broken through a few times.

Sighing wearily, she pushed her troubled thoughts aside and went to bed. Another busy day beckoned in the morning. And it was the dance show at night.

The following day sparked in, and as the late afternoon turned to twilight, Huntine arrived at the theatre and went backstage where Dair, his tour director, the other dancers, and others were all abuzz, getting ready for the opening night. Cambeul wasn't there as he was attending to the play's second night's performance.

Dair wore his costume, the ghillie shirt and trews, and his makeup was done. He came striding over to welcome her.

'All set?' he said.

'Yes, I'd better get my makeup done and costume ready.' As she said this, she was swept away to have her hair and makeup done along with some of the others.

Dair felt that he wasn't getting a chance to talk to her properly. But in the whirlwind of getting ready for the show, there was no time to chat. Everyone was buzzing around, and the audience were starting to arrive. From backstage, he could hear the chatter as they settled in their seats. All tickets had sold.

'We've got a full house tonight,' the tour director said to Dair.

'There's a great atmosphere,' Dair observed, peering round the curtain, taking a peek as the large auditorium started to fill up.

'Jock's here with Jessy,' the tour director told him. 'And Mullcairn and his girlfriend. I like the idea of them all coming up on to the stage to dance with you and Huntine.'

'Surely it's only Jock and Jessy.'

'My mistake, sorry, Dair. When I sent the complimentary tickets to Mullcairn that included backstage passes, I told him he'd be invited up on stage for a wee dance. He sounded delighted. He says he's wearing his kilt.'

'Don't tell Mullcairn about the mix up. He can come up with the others and dance.'

'Aye, it'll be fun.' The tour director checked the time. 'I'd better start getting everyone ready.' He hurried away, and Dair joined him, helping to make sure the show started on time.

Dair tried to talk to Huntine, but in the melee backstage, he kept getting waylaid by others. But his heart took a hit seeing how gorgeous she looked with her stage makeup on and wearing one of the dresses.

Then it was time for him to take his place beside the piano, and play the opening riff on the guitar for the first song.

Huntine stood on stage with the other dancers, performing while Dair sang and played the piano and guitar.

Dair was surprised to hear members of the audience singing along and moving to the beat of his song.

Then Dair joined in the dance routine. He danced solo, and then partnered with Huntine. Sparks charged between them, and it was one of those nights when the energy of the dance, the entertainment, lifted everyone's performance.

The lighting was fantastic, creating a wonderful atmosphere on stage, and Huntine's costumes were beautiful. She was beautiful, Dair thought, as he danced with her.

Wearing Shona's purple dress, Huntine performed the lively number with Dair that was packed with lifts. The audience loved it, and cheered when they performed.

'The atmosphere is electric!' Dair said to Huntine as they hurried backstage for a quick costume change while the other dancers performed.

'I've never felt anything like this,' she said.

Now back and ready to perform the next number, Huntine wore the sparkling tartan ensemble to dance the Highland Fling that Dair had choreographed with a medley of other movements. He wore his kilt, and they danced front of stage together.

Gazing out at the audience while she danced, she saw her grandparents waving, and beside them was Mullcairn waving too.

As they finished, it was straight into another costume change and then back on to tackle the tango. The dancers were paired up, all in tango outfits, and the music was dramatic.

Huntine wore the red dress and Latin shoes with heels. Intertwining with Dair, it was a dance of passion, and again the connection between them created a powerful performance.

Dair had taken Cambeul's advice and moved the tango to the last dance before the interval.

After the interval, Dair invited the selected members of the audience to come up on stage.

'And we have popular radio presenter, Mullcairn, with us tonight,' Dair announced, and the audience clapped as he swaggered up on to the stage wearing his kilt, and brought Etta with him.

'Come on, Jessy,' Jock whispered to her, taking her by surprise.

'I thought I was dancing on stage with Dair in Glasgow,' said Jessy.

'You are, this is a wee extra treat.'

Jessy's face lit up with joy.

Jock escorted Jessy up. He wore a suit, and Jessy was wearing one of her dance dresses from the past, an elegant mid–length dress that had a scattering of sequins. It was perfect for waltzing. Jessy hardly stopped smiling, loving every moment of dancing on stage with Dair.

'You dance beautifully, Jessy,' Dair told her, impressed by her dancing.

Jessy beamed with delight.

Huntine danced alongside them with Jock, and it truly was a night to remember for all of them together. Mullcairn also danced with Huntine, while Etta danced with Dair.

The audience clearly enjoyed this part of the show, and then the guests went back down to their seats as they second half of the show began with a lively foxtrot and quickstep medley. The dance routines flowed from one to the other, and the audience were entertained from start to finish. The lifts were spectacular, especially the routines where Dair lifted Huntine up in a variety of challenging lifts.

Huntine herself loved the lifts, delighted that all their hard work had paid off, hearing the audience gasp and cheer.

Between the dances, Dair sang and played piano and guitar. He was impressed how well Huntine danced and performed. She wore every dress as planned, from the shimmering silver and silver boa, to the pink, purple and aqua designs.

Then it was time for the closing routines. Huntine emerged from backstage wearing the pink ballgown, sparkling like something out of a fairytale. Dair wore the classic suit, and as he took her in hold he whispered, 'You look beautiful, Huntine.'

She smiled up at him, and they danced to the romantic music, finishing with their stage kiss.

Huntine didn't get it wrong. Neither did Dair. But instead of a stage kiss, Dair gave in to the romance of the moment, held Huntine in his arms and kissed her. Really kissed her.

She felt the loving warmth of Dair's kiss, and gave in to the feelings in her heart too.

The audience cheered, thinking this was part of the performance. Just an act.

'Did Dair really kiss Huntine?' Jessy said to Jock.

Jock nodded and smiled.

'I think we've got a wee romance between Huntine and Dair,' Mullcairn said, joining in the conversation.

Etta agreed. 'They make such a lovely couple.'

The next routine began after the romantic waltz, and included a medley of various types of ballroom and stage dancing.

The dancers then stood at the front of the stage and took a final bow after they'd finished.

The audience applauded and cheered having enjoyed the show.

Jock, Jessy, Mullcairn and Etta, joined Dair and Huntine backstage afterwards. In the merry melee, everyone enjoyed themselves.

Dair also had his special meet and greet backstage with some audience members to chat with them and have photographs taken.

Before they left, Jessy gave Huntine a hug. 'Thank you and Dair for such a wonderful night.' And then she whispered to her. 'We saw Dair kiss you. Are you two having a wee romance?'

'No.' Huntine smiled and hugged Jessy and Jock before they left to have a night at the hotel.

'Listen to my next show,' Mullcairn said to Dair and Huntine. 'I'll give your show a mention and tell folks that I was dancing on the stage.'

'I will,' Dair confirmed.

'I'll be sure to listen in,' Huntine promised.

Waving, Mullcairn and Etta headed away.

As the dancers packed up and started to head home, Dair took a moment to talk to Huntine.

'You were outstanding tonight. A beautiful dancer,' he said.

'I loved it. But I still think I belong in my world of writing. Though it's a night to remember.'

'I'll never forget it. And I'll never forget you,' he told her. 'What are your plans now? When are you leaving?'

'Probably tomorrow, but soon. I've things to sort out, and then I'll drive back to Glasgow.'

He took a deep breath. 'Is there any chance you could change your mind, and stay in Edinburgh?'

She shook her head. 'No.'

'I'll miss you, Huntine Grey.'

'I'll miss you too, Dair. But we'll keep in touch.' She didn't sound hopeful that they would. Their wonderful, wild and exciting time together seemed over, and things could easily drift, as so often happened in her world.

Dair went to talk to her some more, but he was interrupted by his tour director bursting to tell him the news. 'Shona won! Shona and her partner won the competition!'

Huntine was delighted, but as Dair and the tour director chatted about this, she left quietly, heading out to the theatre's foyer.

Her phone rang, and she saw that it was Cambeul. He was smiling at her from the phone. He'd taken his tie off and the top buttons of his shirt were undone. 'Shona has accepted the role for the Christmas play!'

'That's wonderful,' Huntine told him.

'Sorry, Shona's phoning,' he said excitedly. 'I have to take this.'

Huntine smiled and let Cambeul chat happily to Shona, and walked out of the theatre and drove home.

After the next night's performance at the theatre in Edinburgh, Dair went home and tried to unwind. He'd showered and changed into a pair of dark trousers and threw on a white shirt. He didn't even bother buttoning it. His guts were still twisted in knots, missing Huntine, and resisting phoning her. He had to let her go, and yet...

Dair opened the patio doors wide, letting the warm night air in, sat down at his piano and began to play.

The hand–written sheet music for his unfinished song was propped up, and he played what he'd written. He'd recently added to it, feeling he now had the right words. It was finished now. He'd struggled to find the right title for the song, but kept coming back to one, though he risked it breaking his heart every time he'd have to play the song.

As the music resonated through the living room and out into the night air, he didn't hear Huntine arrive.

She followed the music.

Dair played the beautiful melody, but then something made him look up and there she was, standing outside in the garden wearing her turquoise dress. His heart thundered in anticipation as she walked towards the open patio doors.

'I changed my mind.' Her words drifted into the night air, and reached deep into his heart.

Dair stood up and hurried over to her, his unbuttoned shirt wafting openly. But then he stopped, wondering if he was hearing right.

'I'm not leaving Edinburgh,' she clarified. 'I'm staying here for a wee while longer.'

'How long?' he said, daring to hope.

Huntine gazed up at the starry sky. 'It'll probably be snowing by the time I leave.'

'No one wants to leave Edinburgh when it's snowing. The city is too beautiful in winter. And you certainly don't want to leave in the spring when the trees are covered in pink blossom. It's so pretty.'

'That's true.' She stepped inside the living room and now gazed up at him.

'You could be here for a while.'

'There's every chance. But I'm taking a chance, risking a broken heart.'

Dair stepped closer. 'I'll never break your heart, Huntine. Your heart will always be safe with me.' He moved closer, gazing down at her with his gorgeous blue eyes. 'I've been falling in love with you since the day we first met.'

'I've been falling in love with you too, Dair.'

He pulled her close, leaned down and kissed her, soft and gentle, and then with all the passion and the romance he felt for her.

Huntine felt herself drop her guard completely. She did feel safe in the arms of this wonderful loving man.

They stepped back to catch their breath.

'What made you change your mind?' he said.

'A few things...I'll be working on the new autumn play with Cambeul, and the Christmas play. But I'm a wordsmith. I can write anywhere, so I'd have to say, it was *you*.'

He smiled at her.

'I've extended the lease on my flat,' she told him. 'I love the view of Edinburgh from my window when I'm writing. And I have a friend now. He has a lovely garden where I can pop over and write outside in the sunlight.'

'Whenever you want,' he assured her.

Huntine started to feel at home. An exciting home, filled with joy and potential.

'We can make this work,' he said.

'I'll stay here in Edinburgh sometimes while you're touring, but I'll come along to a lot of the performances when the play is showing in the same city or town. And it's only an hour and a half drive to Glasgow for the shows there.'

'It'll be a whirlwind of a summer, but such an exciting time,' he said, smiling.

'We'll have to juggle things around sometimes to make it work.'

'We're both in the entertainment business.'

'We are.'

They smiled at each other, and then he wrapped her in his arms and kissed her until they were both breathless and smiling and filled with hope of a new life together.

When he finally let her go, she noticed the sheet music propped up on his piano stand. And blinked, reading the title of his new song. She looked at Dair for an explanation.

'I realised why I could never finish this song, until now. I hadn't met you.'

'Play it for me.'

Dair sat down at the piano and began to play the song, entitled — *Huntine*.

It's the last song
The last dance
But it's the start of our romance
Writing and dancing
It was meant to be
I'm in love with you
You're in love with me
I promise I'll love you forever
Romance and dancing together...

End

About the Author:

De-ann Black is a bestselling author, scriptwriter and former newspaper journalist. She has over 100 books published. Romance, thrillers, espionage novels, action adventure. And children's books (non-fiction rocket science books and children's fiction). She became an Amazon All-Star author in 2014 and 2015.

She previously worked as a full-time newspaper journalist for several years. She had her own weekly columns in the press. This included being a motoring correspondent where she got to test drive cars every week for the press for three years.

Before being asked to work for the press, De-ann worked in magazine editorial writing everything from fashion features to social news. She was the marketing editor of a glossy magazine.

She is also a professional artist and illustrator. Embroidery design, fabric design, dressmaking, sewing, knitting and fashion are part of her work.

Additionally, De-ann has always been interested in fitness, and was a fitness and bodybuilding champion, 100 metre runner and mountaineer. As a former N.A.B.B.A. Miss Scotland, she had a weekly fitness show on the radio that ran for over three years.

De-ann trained in Shukokai karate, boxing, kickboxing, Dayan Qigong and Jiu Jitsu. She is currently based in Scotland.

Her 16 colouring books are available in paperback, including her latest Summer Nature Colouring Book and Flower Nature Colouring Book.

Her latest embroidery pattern books include: Floral Garden Embroidery Patterns, Christmas & Winter Embroidery Patterns, Floral Spring Embroidery Patterns and Sea Theme Embroidery Patterns.

Website: Find out more at: www.de-annblack.com

Fabric, Wallpaper & Home Decor Collections:
De-ann's fabric designs and wallpaper collections, and home decor items, including her popular Scottish Garden Thistles patterns, are available from Spoonflower.
www.de-annblack.com/spoonflower

Also by De-ann Black (Romance, Action/Thrillers & Children's books). See her Amazon Author page or website for further details about her books, screenplays, illustrations, art, fabric designs and embroidery patterns.

Amazon Author page:
www.De-annBlack.com/Amazon

Romance books:

Dance, Music & Scottish Romance series:
1. Romance Dancer

Quilt Shop by the Seaside
Embroidery Bee

Scottish Loch Romance series:
1. Sewing & Mending Cottage
2. Scottish Loch Summer Romance
3. Sweet Music
4. Knitting Bee
5. Autumn Romance
6. Christmas Ballroom Dancing
7. Scottish Highlands New Year Ball
8. Crafting Bee: Crafts & Romance in Scotland

Music, Dance & Romance series:
1. The Sweetest Waltz
2. Knitting & Starlight
3. Ballroom Dancing Christmas Romance

Snow Bells Haven series:
1. Snow Bells Christmas
2. Snow Bells Wedding
3. Love & Lyrics

The Cure for Love Romance series:
1. The Cure for Love
2. The Cure for Love at Christmas

Scottish Highlands & Island Romance series:
1. Scottish Island Knitting Bee
2. Scottish Island Fairytale Castle
3. Vintage Dress Shop on the Island
4. Fairytale Christmas on the Island
5. Summer Ball Weddings & Waltzing

Quilting Bee & Tea Shop series:
1. The Quilting Bee
2. The Tea Shop by the Sea
3. Embroidery Cottage
4. Knitting Shop by the Sea
5. Christmas Weddings

Sewing, Crafts & Quilting series:
1. The Sewing Bee
2. The Sewing Shop
3. Knitting Cottage (Scottish Highland romance)
4. Scottish Highlands Christmas Wedding

Cottages, Cakes & Crafts series:
1. The Flower Hunter's Cottage
2. The Sewing Bee by the Sea
3. The Beemaster's Cottage
4. The Chocolatier's Cottage
5. The Bookshop by the Seaside
6. The Dressmaker's Cottage

Scottish Chateau, Colouring & Crafts series:
1. Christmas Cake Chateau
2. Colouring Book Cottage

Summer Sewing Bee

Sewing, Knitting & Baking series:
1. The Tea Shop
2. The Sewing Bee & Afternoon Tea
3. The Christmas Knitting Bee
4. Champagne Chic Lemonade Money
5. The Vintage Sewing & Knitting Bee

Tea Dress Shop series:
1. The Tea Dress Shop At Christmas
2. The Fairytale Tea Dress Shop In Edinburgh
3. The Vintage Tea Dress Shop In Summer

The Tea Shop & Tearoom series:
1. The Christmas Tea Shop & Bakery
2. The Christmas Chocolatier
3. The Chocolate Cake Shop in New York at Christmas
4. The Bakery by the Seaside
5. Shed in the City

Christmas Romance series:
1. Christmas Romance in Paris
2. Christmas Romance in Scotland

Oops! I'm the Paparazzi series:
1. Oops! I'm the Paparazzi
2. Oops! I'm Up To Mischief
3. Oops! I'm the Paparazzi, Again

The Bitch-Proof Suit series:
1. The Bitch-Proof Suit
2. The Bitch-Proof Romance
3. The Bitch-Proof Bride
4. The Bitch-Proof Wedding

Heather Park: Regency Romance
Dublin Girl
Why Are All The Good Guys Total Monsters?
I'm Holding Out For A Vampire Boyfriend

Action/Thriller books:

Knight in Miami

Agency Agenda

Love Him Forever

Someone Worse

Electric Shadows

The Strife Of Riley

Shadows Of Murder

Cast a Dark Shadow

Children's books:

Faeriefied

Secondhand Spooks

Poison-Wynd

Wormhole Wynd

Science Fashion

School For Aliens

Colouring books:

Summer Nature

Flower Nature

Summer Garden

Spring Garden

Autumn Garden

Sea Dream

Festive Christmas

Christmas Garden

Christmas Theme

Flower Bee

Wild Garden

Faerie Garden Spring

Flower Hunter

Stargazer Space

Bee Garden

Scottish Garden Seasons

Embroidery Design books:

Floral Garden Embroidery Patterns

Floral Spring Embroidery Patterns

Christmas & Winter Embroidery Patterns

Sea Theme Embroidery Patterns

Floral Nature Embroidery Designs

Scottish Garden Embroidery Designs

Printed in Dunstable, United Kingdom

63559065R00147